cathy cassidy

Indigo Blue

PUFFIN

PUFFIN BOOKS

Published by the Penguin Group
Penguin Books Ltd, 80 Strand, London WC2R ORL, England
Penguin Group (USA) Inc., 375 Hudson Street, New York, New York 10014, USA
Penguin Group (Canada), 90 Eglinton Avenue East, Suite 700, Toronto, Ontario, Canada M4P 2Y3
(a division of Pearson Penguin Canada Inc.)
Penguin Ireland, 25 St Stephen's Green, Dublin 2, Ireland (a division of Penguin Books Ltd)
Penguin Group (Australia), 250 Camberwell Road, Camberwell, Victoria 3124, Australia
(a division of Pearson Australia Group Pty Ltd)
Penguin Books India Pvt Ltd, 11 Community Centre, Panchsheel Park, New Delhi – 110 017, India
Penguin Group (NZ), cnr Airborne and Rosedale Roads, Albany, Auckland 1310, New Zealand
(a division of Pearson New Zealand Ltd)
Penguin Books (South Africa) (Pty) Ltd, 24 Sturdee Avenue, Rosebank, Johannesburg 2196, South Africa

Penguin Books Ltd, Registered Offices: 80 Strand, London WC2R ORL, England

puffinbooks.com

First published 2005
1

This edition published for The Book People Ltd,
Hall Wood Avenue, Haydock, St Helens, WA11 9UL

Copyright © Cathy Cassidy, 2005
All rights reserved

The moral right of the author has been asserted

Set in 13/16.5 pt Monotype Baskerville
Typeset by Rowland Phototypesetting Ltd, Bury St Edmunds, Suffolk
Made and printed in England by Clays Ltd, St Ives plc

British Library Cataloguing in Publication Data
A CIP catalogue record for this book is available from the British Library

ISBN: 978-1-856-13238-1

www.greenpenguin.co.uk

Penguin Books is committed to a sustainable future
for our business, our readers and our planet.
The book in your hands is made from paper
certified by the Forest Stewardship Council.

Hi there!

It's a typical Scottish summer day here — grey clouds, drizzle, midgies and just a sliver of sunshine peeping through. It's not exactly the Costa del Sol, but who cares?

It's a perfect daydreaming day — and for me, dreaming is just a step away from writing. *Indigo Blue* is my second book, all about a girl called Indie who loves to daydream. When one thing in Indie's life goes pear-shaped, a whole raft of other stuff follows — and no amount of dreaming can fix it all up.

I hope you enjoy *Indigo Blue*. Here's to daydreams, friendship, strawberry laces and hot chocolate with melted marshmallows, which can help you through the worst of times — promise!

Best wishes,

Cathy Cassidy

xxxx

cathycassidy.com

Thanks!

To Liam, for endless encouragement, patience and healthy dinners, and to Cal and Caitlin for their inspiration, enthusiasm and ability to survive on cheese butties and loud music when things get seriously busy. Thanks to Catriona, fab first-reader, and to Mum, Dad, Andy, Lori, Joan, Mary-Jane, Fiona, Helen, Sheena, Martyn, Zarah and all my wonderful friends for the support, the pep-talks, the shopping trips and the chocolate. Also to Paul, for creating such a cool website for me.

Thanks to Tallulah and Roxanne, *Indigo Blue*'s first 'real' readers, and to the best ever agent, Darley Anderson, for believing in it all. Big hugs all round to Rebecca, Francesca, Adele, Nick, Shannon and the whole Puffin team for making it happen, and to Julia and Lucie at the agency. Who says dreams don't come true?

I'm never late for school.

I leave home around eight o'clock on a school-day morning, even though it only takes five minutes on the bus, fifteen if I'm walking. And that's if I'm walking slowly, maybe stopping at Singhs for a penny chew or a look at the comics.

I'm almost always the first person to get here, even before Billy, the janitor, who comes at half eight to open up. Sometimes he lets me in for a warm by the big old-fashioned radiators, but mostly I just sit on the little wall at the edge of the playground and dream.

My friend Jo goes to gymnastics and swimming club. She reads teen magazines and scary books and collects beanie animals and she's learning to play the violin. She has loads of hobbies. I don't do all that stuff – my only real hobby is daydreaming. It's something that never lets you down, because

I

it's free and it's easy and I'm in charge of what happens.

Sometimes I sit on the wall and imagine that this is the day the circus will come to town, right into the school playground. Acrobats, trapeze artistes and clowns will cartwheel and strut across the footy pitch. We'll all learn to paint our faces, ride a unicycle and balance on one leg on a galloping horse – better than fractions, spelling tests and getting picked last for the netball team.

Sometimes I dream that school is cancelled due to freak floods or blizzards, or that we all get stranded in class for weeks on end and have to be rescued by soldiers in boats or helicopters or dog sleds. Sometimes I imagine I've won a national competition for painting or acting or inventing a car that runs on orange juice and recycled sweet wrappers, and even Miss McDougall thinks I'm sussed and cool and dripping with talent.

My favourite daydream is about my dad. He comes driving into the playground in an indigo-blue Ferrari and squeals to a halt right in front of me. He leans over to open the passenger door and I can see him clearly – sometimes he's a cooler, fairer version of Robbie Williams, and other times he looks just like Mr Lennon, our head teacher, only not so podgy.

He smiles at me and it makes up for the whole of

the last eleven years. I get into the passenger seat and we speed right out of that playground while everyone stands and stares, and I remember to send postcards to them all from New York, Cairo, Mexico City and our lush private villa in the Bahamas.

Well, maybe.

After half eight, kids start arriving at school, a few at a time. Some come with mums and pushchairs and squirmy baby brothers and sisters. Some come by car, some come by bus, some come on bikes, and Shane Taggart comes on his skate-board, every day, except when it snows.

Jo gets here at five to nine most days. She's been my best mate since we met on the very first day of school. She never laughed at my hair, which was all blonde dreadlocks and multi-coloured beads and feathers. She never asked why I was wearing an ancient turquoise felted jumper and tie-dyed leggings instead of a blue polo top and navy pinafore dress. She just raised her eyebrows, giggled and dragged me off to the sandpit.

I'm eleven now, and I know way more about fitting in. I got my mum to chop out all the dread-locks when I was in Year Two – she still has them in a wooden box, along with her photos and her hippy jewellery and a yellowed ticket for Glastonbury Festival from hundreds of years ago.

I looked like a scarecrow for a whole year while my hair grew out, and ever since then I've looked after it myself – one hundred brush-strokes every night, conditioner every time I wash it, cute hair-clips and tiny plaits and zigzag partings and little twisty buns with the ends sticking out, the way they do it in Jo's magazines.

I'm pretty much in charge of my own clothes too. Gran gets me basic uniform stuff every August and Mum lets me choose a few cool tops, some clumpy shoes or a little skirt to liven it all up. Sometimes they come from the charity shop, but I don't care about that as long as nobody at school catches on.

I look like the other kids, and that's what matters.

I've changed, and not just the way I look but the way I feel inside too. It might be something to do with growing up, but it's probably more to do with Mum and Max and Misti and all that stuff.

At least Jo never changes.

When things have been bad at home, she pretends not to notice. Jo doesn't ask awkward questions or try to get deep and meaningful. She doesn't do slushy and she doesn't do sad. She just rolls her eyes, digs me in the ribs and tells me silly stories and corny jokes, and we link arms and laugh and talk and the bad thoughts go away.

Last night was bad.

Mum and Max were shouting downstairs for hours and hours, and then they moved up to their room and the shouting got louder so that hiding under the covers and turning my CD player up to full volume didn't help any more.

Misti, who has the box room next to me, started crying around midnight and nobody came to see to her. I wrapped myself in the duvet and crept across the landing, and even in the dark I could see she was standing up in her cot, her face streaked with tears.

I scooped her up in my arms, my little sister who's only just two, and I tried not to hear the things that Max was screaming at my mum because you're not meant to know words like that when you're only eleven.

I climbed back into bed with my arms round Misti, singing corny pop songs into her hair and wiping her eyes with the duvet cover.

After a while everything went quiet – I suppose Mum and Max were making up. They usually do, kind of. It's just that it never lasts for long.

And, after that, Misti stopped snuffling and drifted off to sleep, her breath a soft whisper on my neck.

I heard footsteps on the landing, water running in the bathroom, stairs creaking. Someone was moving around downstairs, but quietly.

I don't remember falling asleep, but I wake up dead on half seven, like I always do. There might as well be an invisible alarm clock inside my head.

I leave Misti cocooned in the duvet and roll out of bed. The house is silent as I wash and brush my teeth. I dress in yesterday's skirt with a fresh top, clean undies and black tights with a darn that hardly shows just behind the knee.

I tiptoe down the stairs and past the living-room door. It's ajar, and inside I see Mum curled up on the sofa asleep, her Chinese robe wrapped round her instead of a blanket. There are bulging bin bags all around the room, and a few things don't look right.

The fringed Indian hanging with all the tiny mirrors is gone from the wall, and so are the framed photos of Misti and me. The stripy rug has disappeared, and the bookshelves look half empty.

Spring-cleaning in the middle of the night is not a good plan. I hope Mum susses that when she wakes up.

I make toast and drink the last of the orange juice from the fridge. I do it silently because I don't want to wake Mum.

I brush my hair, push in some glittery clips and grab my school bag from behind the door. I pull on my fleece and root around for a hat because it's raining hard outside, and I haven't any money for bus fare today.

I'm almost out of the door when Max comes down.

He's tall and fair and rumpled-looking with big sad eyes, and when Mum first met him three years ago she said he was the best-looking man she'd ever seen. He was kind and funny and generous then, and we had lots of laughs, the three of us.

Max isn't laughing now.

He's wearing jeans but his feet and chest are bare, and his blond hair is sticking up like he's been sleeping in a hedge. He comes closer and I can smell the drink on him: stale beer, sweat, sadness.

He doesn't look like a man who's been shouting, screaming and swearing all night, he just looks crushed, lost, hopeless.

'Indie,' he says. 'Indie, you have to talk to your mum.'

I pull on a blue fleece hat with long tassels and refuse to look at him.

'She's going to leave me,' Max says. 'She doesn't love me any more. You have to stop her, Indie. Tell her she can't do it.'

'I'll try,' I mutter, dragging open the front door. I step out into the rain, but he's following me, and I can see tears in his eyes.

I've never seen a man cry before.

'Indie, please,' he says raggedly. 'Please. Talk to her.'

He catches hold of my arm and holds me tight. I can't tell whether it's rain or tears on my face.

'We've been happy, haven't we?' Max asks. 'We've had good times. Tell her I'm sorry, Indie. I love her. I do. You have to make her see!'

His fingers dig into my arm, but he doesn't mean to hurt me. It's because he's upset.

'Max . . .'

'Let her go.'

It's Mum, standing in the doorway, her Chinese silk wrap pulled tight round her, fair hair falling loose across her face.

'*Take – your – hands – off – my – daughter.*'

Her voice is hard and slow and fierce and determined. Max lets his hand fall away from

8

my arm, and suddenly he looks lost and alone, standing in the rain without his shirt, without his shoes, on the path of the little house we've all called home for three years.

'Indie, I'm sorry . . .'

'Get away from her,' Mum says, and Max slinks back inside like a naughty schoolboy.

I turn away, put my hand on the gate.

'Indie, babe.' Mum is next to me now, but I daren't look up.

'It's going to be all right from now on. I'm going to fix it, sort things out, get us out of here.'

'What?'

'Don't worry, love, I'll put things right. We'll be OK, just the three of us: me, you, Misti. Wait for me after school, Indie. I'll fetch you. Wait for me. Only don't come back here, d'you understand?'

'I understand.'

For a long, long moment our eyes lock, and although I try not to notice I can't help but see the blue-black bruises on Mum's face. The bruises that weren't there yesterday.

3

By the time I get to school I'm drenched, and I stand in the porch for ages before Billy arrives and opens up. He lets me in and I arrange my hat and fleece on the big cast-iron radiator, steaming.

I sit cross-legged with my back against the radiator to dry out, my hair hanging in rat's tails on my shoulders.

Billy slips me a snack-sized Mars bar, shaking his head.

I need a seriously brilliant daydream today, one that can blot out the memory of Mum's face and Max's tears, and the sick sense that something weird and scary is going on. I just can't do it, though, so I hug my legs and press my face into my knees and blank it all out – the drumming of the rain outside, the swish of the door and the giggles and shouts as kids start arriving, the off-tune whistling from down the corridor where Billy is doing something complicated to the broken door latch on Class Six.

'OK, Indie?'

Jo scuffs a toe against my soggy trainers, grinning.

I jump up and we link arms, and it's OK again. All the home stuff fades out and I'm safe and sure and happy. Pretty much.

We mooch off together to watch out for Shane Taggart, Jo's latest crush. Just before nine, he skids into the playground on his skateboard and rolls to a halt in front of the doors, flicking his board upright and winking at us. Jo goes pink and pretends to be looking somewhere else completely. I stifle a yawn.

Sadly, it's all downhill from there. I get a row from Miss McDougall for forgetting my English book, then I bomb out with a measly 4/20 in the mental maths test after break. Worst of all, Miss McDougall homes right in while we're getting changed for PE and asks me how I hurt my arm. I tell her some junk about banging it in the play-ground yesterday, but when I look down I can see that it looks like exactly what it is: a ring of dark bruises where somebody's held on to me way too hard. Thanks a bunch, Max.

So Miss McDougall gives me a long, funny look, then puts a hand on my shoulder and says, 'Indigo, is everything OK at home?' I go kind of pink and shake off her hand and say everything is fine. As if I'd tell *her* anything.

Only now Jo is looking at me sort of weird too, which bugs me loads, because I need today to be normal and ordinary and totally pity-free.

Sadly, it's not happening.

Jo asks if I want to come over to her place for tea, and of course I have to tell her that I can't.

'Why can't you?' she wants to know.

I don't go over to hers that often because she has a whole raft of things to do most days – violin lessons and gym and swimming club and stuff – only sometimes her mum loosens up a bit and I get an invite. I always go, because unlike Jo *I'm* never doing anything after school. Mum doesn't mind as long as I ring and let her know, and as long as Jo's mum drops me back before seven or so.

'I just can't,' I mutter.

'But why?' Jo pushes. 'Is something up?'

'No. I'm busy after school, that's all.'

Miss McDougall tells us off for talking when we should be practising our handstands, and gives us twenty sit-ups apiece as punishment. Jo is not impressed.

Coming back from the gym hall, I notice she's sulking. She manages to keep it up till lunch, then, watching me push cold macaroni cheese around my plate, she finally cracks.

'Why are you so secretive?' she explodes. 'You're meant to be my best mate, only you never tell me anything. I only asked you over cos you looked so down today. I wanted to cheer you up.'

'I'm OK,' I say helplessly.

'You are not. You've been biting your nails all morning. Your eyes are all red and puffy too. And your arm . . .'

'I banged it yesterday!' I snap.

'Yeah, right. Look, Indie, if you don't want to be my friend, just say so . . .'

Great. How did we get to this, on top of every-thing else? Just because I can't go to hers for tea.

We mooch up to the counter for dishes of apple pie and lumpy custard. I slump back into my seat.

'I am your friend. Honest. And I'd love to come to tea, really I would, only I just can't, not tonight.'

'Why not?'

I push my dish away and let out a long, raggedy sigh. I can see this conversation going round and round in circles for hours, days, weeks even. Jo is not going to let go.

Across the table, Aisha Patel is giving me a long, sad-eyed look too, which is the last thing I need.

I can just imagine their faces if I tell them what's really going on. Even the edited highlights don't bear thinking about. On the other hand, it's not the sort of thing you can hide for long . . .

'I think we're moving house,' I say.

There's a silence. Aisha's eyes go all huge and anxious. Jo, by contrast, is frowning.

'Moving?' she says. 'You can't be. You've only been there a couple of years. Hasn't Max just put in a new kitchen? It's dead nice, your house. Anyway, you can't be moving, not today. You never even mentioned it before.'

'It was sort of a last-minute decision.'

'Oh, sure.'

'Honest, Jo. I have to wait for Mum after school. She said. So I can't come over to yours, not tonight.'

'Fine,' says Jo. 'Suit yourself.'

More silence.

Aisha makes an attempt to lighten the mood. 'Where are you moving to?' she asks.

'Yeah,' chips in Jo. 'Where are you moving to?'

How d'you answer that one?

'I don't know,' I admit at last.

4

The last bell goes on possibly my worst ever day at school since the time in Year Two I was sick all over myself at the dinner table and had to lie down in the office, wearing a nylon stripy T-shirt and an enormous pair of grey flannel boys' shorts from around about the time of Noah's Ark.

No, seriously, this is worse.

On the day I need her to be fun and easy and no questions asked, Jo has been anxious, pitying, paranoid, sulky and downright nosey. And now she thinks I'm telling her lies and she's walking home with Aisha Patel.

I sit on the wall and watch the kids scatter, mums and snotty baby brothers and sisters in tow. The playground's quiet now, except for some Year Three lads from down the road kicking a ball around in the corner.

I look at my watch. Mum's only ten minutes late, so I don't have to worry or anything. She's probably been dead busy. She'll be here pretty soon and it'll all get sorted – she'll explain about this morning, make everything OK.

Maybe I got it wrong, the moving stuff. Maybe she and Max have made it up, and he'll trundle up in his flash blue builder's van and we'll all head off to get a big chip supper and maybe go watch a film, the way we used to before Misti was born.

We were happy then.

And it's not like things arc awful or anything now, not all the time anyway. Like Jo said, Max is always fixing up the house. He put in this new kitchen before Christmas, and last year he made a patio and bought a barbecue for the back garden. Mum planted a whole load of flowers and it looked so cool, like something off one of those garden programmes.

Moving is definitely a bad idea. In some ways.

If it stops the rows, though, that has to be good. Did they row right back at the start, before Misti was born? I can't remember for sure, but I know that things have been worse this last year or two. It's Mum's fault, a lot of it – that's what she says, anyhow.

I know she's forgetful, because she sometimes forgets to put sugar in Max's tea or makes lentil soup when she knows Max needs a proper dinner after a hard day's work. Sometimes, she even forgets to keep the dinner hot when he comes home late, or worse, she lets it burn.

That makes Max mad, like when Misti has left her toys strewn about in the living room, or when she's been messing with the stuff in the bathroom and tearing up loo roll or making bubbles to wash her doll in the sink. It's Mum's fault that Max gets angry, because sometimes she forgets to check that everything is OK.

Mum's clumsy too – maybe it goes with being forgetful. She walked into a door once, she said, and she's slipped over on the ice a couple of times and got bruised pretty badly. She trips over Misti sometimes, or forgets about the dodgy door on the high kitchen cupboard and grazes her face.

'Oh, Indie,' she says, whenever that happens. 'What am I like? I could fall off my own two feet! I must be the clumsiest person ever. Hopeless!' And she laughs and bites her lip and takes the concealer out of her bag to hide the bruise on her cheek, the black eye, the cut lip.

Mum should be more careful. She should remember to keep the house tidy, keep Misti quiet, make the kind of food Max likes. If she did all that, and took care not to be clumsy too, then maybe the rows would ease up.

Sometimes, though, when Mum and Max argue and shout and scream, I wonder if it's anything to do with being forgetful and clumsy. I wonder if maybe, sometimes, it might just be about Max.

'Everything OK, Indigo?'

Everything is far from OK when Miss McDougall is creeping up behind me, looking at me all worried and faintly disapproving.

'Fine, Miss,' I say brightly.

'Are you waiting for someone?'

'My mum, Miss.'

Miss McDougall frowns at her watch. 'She seems rather late. Would you like me to call home for you?'

'No, Miss. Thank you, Miss, but she's not at home. She said she might be late. Everything's fine, Miss, really.'

'Very well, Indigo, but if there's a problem . . . look, I'll just give you some money for the phone. Or for bus fare, just in case.'

'Thanks, Miss.'

I put the coins in my pocket ready to give back to her tomorrow morning. We don't take hand-outs, Mum's always made that clear, but Miss McDougall is only trying to be kind.

I watch her big tweedy figure trail across the playground into the staff car-parking area. She gives me a wave as she vrooms away.

Miss McDougall is strict, but she means well.

It's just that she's not the kind of teacher you can really talk to.

Jo's magazines are always advising you to talk things through with a trusted adult. The problem is, I don't trust that many adults. Maybe Gran, but she's miles away, in Wales.

And maybe Mrs Keenan, who was my teacher in Reception. She was so kind and patient and smiley, and she seemed to like everybody for what they were, no matter what. Sometimes, when I got to hold her hand walking up and down to the gym hall or the lunch room or the music hut, she'd kind of squeeze my fingers gently in hers and make me feel all warm and safe and good. I thought it was a secret sign between the two of us, something special. It was years before I realized she did the same thing to everyone.

Mrs Keenan still smiles at me if we pass in the corridor or the playground, but she's squeezed the hands of hundreds of Reception kids since me. She probably wouldn't even remember my name.

The playground is empty now. The Year Three kids must have headed off while I was dreaming. It's cold, but at least it's not raining. And Mum is very late.

Maybe I got it all wrong this morning, about waiting at the school. Maybe I should just go home like I do every other day.

I won't, though, I know.

I take out my maths book and doodle my way through a page of homework. It's probably mostly wrong, but then hey, what's new about that?

I'm starving. I fish around in my school bag and find Billy's Mars bar from this morning. I scoff it in three bites, making each mouthful last for the count of a hundred.

Then I take some time picturing our new house. It's a tiny cottage with roses round the door, I decide, just big enough for the three of us. Or a cool flat with loads of chrome and leather and soft sheepskin rugs on pale, sanded floorboards. Why not?

I'm all out of daydreams by the time Mum arrives. I'm cold, hungry and scared, but Mum looks so tired and sad that I'm not about to complain. Misti's asleep in the pushchair, her face stained with dirt and tears, and I know that if my day's been bad, theirs has been way beyond.

'Come on, Indie,' Mum says.

I stand up, dragging my rucksack on, pulling the blue fleece hat down over my ears. We trail along in silence, because there isn't a lot to say – it's happened, it's awful, and words won't change any of it.

Besides, Mum's biting her lip in an awful,

trembly kind of way that makes me think she's going to cry if I say anything, anything at all.

We are not heading for home. We walk along Calder's Lane and down behind the factory and then we cut across a big, sprawling estate where some of the houses have boarded-up windows and graffiti on the walls.

I daren't ask how far it is, but it's getting dark now, and I haven't a clue where we are. Miles and miles from school, anyway. Miles and miles from Max.

We pass a row of shops, mostly shut except for a bright, noisy chippy that smells so good my stomach aches with hunger.

Mum pauses on the corner, looking back towards the lights, the smell of hot fat and sharp vinegar. 'Are you hungry?' she asks, frowning. 'Will we get some chips for tea?'

So I go inside and queue for ages and come out with two steaming packages of fish 'n' chips. We stash them in the tray under Misti's buggy and on we go again, drawing deep breaths of the hot, chippy aroma.

'So,' Mum says as we turn at last into a wide, gloomy street, 'I hope you're going to like it. The house is quite big and the rent was very reasonable ... the landlady lives on the ground floor and the rest of the house is divided into flats and rented out. It needs some work, but we can fix it up, can't we?'

'Sure.'

My heart sinks as we walk along Hartington Drive. The houses are big and they must have been posh once, like about a million years ago. Not now.

Number 33 looks like something out of *The Addams Family*. It's tall and crumbly and ancient, with peeling paint on the window frames and dead shrubs in the flower beds. A red Fiat is parked on the drive in front, two mountain bikes are rusting quietly against the wall and the wheelie bins have fallen over by the gate, spilling rubbish on to the pavement.

'This is it, then,' Mum says.

A yellowed curtain twitches and the front door creaks open slowly. A tall, skinny, ancient woman appears on the step and looks down at us like we're something you'd wipe off your shoe.

'Everything settled?' she asks in a tight, dis-approving voice. 'I noticed you moving your things earlier. I must say I didn't think you'd be in quite so quickly. Do you have everything you need?'

'Oh, yes, Mrs Green. We'll soon get everything nice and cosy, don't worry. This is just the place we were looking for.'

Mrs Green looks sceptical. Her eyes skim over

Mum's face, lingering on the vivid bruises that even a heavy layer of make-up can't disguise. She purses her lips.

Mum's beautiful blonde hair is all scraped back hastily into a wispy plait, her blue cord coat has frayed wrists and the hem dips slightly over her navy tie-dyed skirt. Her blue suede boots have a nasty greyish stain all down one side that may or may not have something to do with Misti. Mrs Green is clearly unimpressed.

Misti wakes up and starts to squirm.

'That child needs a bath, a hot meal and an early night,' Mrs Green says curtly. 'You're paid up till the end of the month, but the rent is due again on the first. Don't forget, now.'

'We won't, Mrs Green.'

She shuts the door firmly, leaving us stranded on the gravel, Misti snivelling now, me open-mouthed.

'What a cow!' I breathe. 'What a horrible, nasty, mean-minded old bat!'

'That's our landlady,' Mum says mildly. 'We'll have to get used to her.'

5

I'm freezing.

Misti has stolen most of the duvet and bundled the rest of it over my head. I'm all stuffy and muffled but my bum, legs and toes feel like they're made out of ice. I wriggle and squirm and tug the duvet down, and it's much warmer. Kind of warm and damp.

There's a huge, soggy puddle of sheet all round Misti's curled-up body. Warm, wet and niffy. Mum must have forgotten to change her nappy last night, because she's leaked all over the bed.

I crawl out from under the covers and huddle on the floorboards, shivering. I look around for yesterday's clothes and realize I'm still wearing them, only damper and more crumpled.

A weak spring sun is shining through the curtainless window and I don't have to check my watch to know it's way past half seven. Way past nine, in fact. I am late for school.

I don't even care.

My face feels stiff and grimy because I didn't wash last night – we only had cold water and Mum forgot to pack the soap. My hair feels stringy and tangled and I'm so tired I could sleep for a week.

Mum is asleep in the living room, curled up on my old beanbag with her jacket pulled round her for warmth. She didn't bring her duvet, because it was Max's too, she said, and that wouldn't have been fair.

Last night we rolled out the big stripy rug, but it looks lost on the vast expanse of creaky floor-boards. Bin bags line the sides of the room, and I start rustling through them as quietly as I can in search of clean clothes. Mum's clothes, Misti's clothes, a bag full of shoes and wellies, another stuffed with paperbacks, another with Misti's toys. I find a bag with my stuff in and dredge up knickers, socks, jeans and a jumper. No point looking for school clothes, because I'm not going. Not today.

Not ever again if I have my way.

At least not until I've had a chance to think up some story to explain all this, some way to turn it into a great adventure, a mad, daring thing to do instead of an awful, scary nightmare.

Only, deep down, I know I'd rather be in school doing long division and getting *see me* scrawled at the bottom of my spelling test. I'd rather be anywhere than here.

The bathroom is like a walk-in freezer, and there are patches of blue-grey mould scattered across the walls. Lovely.

I peel off my clothes and run the hot tap, in case something magical has happened and the water heated up all on its own in the night. It hasn't. It couldn't, because our electricity isn't on yet – we need something called a powercard and we haven't bought one yet.

So the water is cold, the heaters don't work, the lights don't go on and the cooker sits coldly in the grubby, poky kitchen. Last night we scrabbled around in the dark with candles, eating lukewarm chips straight out of the paper with no ketchup, no salt, no vinegar.

Cold washes are meant to be good for you, though. Mum said so last night. I splash the icy water all over me, squealing with the shock of it, then dry off using my fleece as a towel because I haven't tracked down the bin bag with the bathroom stuff yet.

I don't know if I'm clean exactly, but I'm definitely awake and I'm starving.

I dress quickly and pad back to the living room. There's a brush in my school bag and I drag it through my hair, tugging out the knots. I dig out clean clothes for Misti and spread them on the rug. I root around till I find her nappies at the bottom of one bin bag, and I set one of those out too, along with the wet wipes and the talc.

'You're a good girl, Indie.'

Mum's awake, just, stretching her skinny arms up and yawning. She stands up, squints around, looking as lost as I feel.

'Breakfast?' I suggest. 'We've got cornflakes and I saw the bowls and spoons a minute ago – they're in here.'

Mum looks hopeless. 'No milk,' she says.

'I'll get some,' I offer, even though I've no idea where I can buy milk because I don't know this part of town and, what's more, I don't want to.

'Will you? There's a corner shop down at the other end of the street. I'll get Misti dressed and have a wash and set the table . . .'

'She's wet,' I say.

'Poor love.'

Mum gives me a pound coin and a shaky smile. 'Yesterday was awful, Indie, but we'll be OK,' she says. 'We'll get this place sorted, see if we don't. It's better this way.'

'What about Max?' I make myself ask.

'Max won't find us here,' Mum says firmly. 'We'll be safe. We'll be OK.'

She gives me a quick hug and I see close up how

the bruises are mellowing to a rich, mottled purple, and how her face is streaked with dried tears.

Things might be better, but they don't feel that way. Not yet.

The corner shop is a bit like Singhs, the kind of place that stays open all hours and sells everything you can think of, but for a price. I buy two litres of milk, full cream, and a plump lady with a Scottish accent hands it over and counts out my change. I buy a tube of Smarties for Misti, to cheer her up. In case she feels as bad as I do. I'd get something for me and Mum too, but there's not enough money unless I break into Miss McDougall's emergency bus fare cash, and I'm not about to do that.

'No school today?' asks the Scottish lady as I turn to go.

'No. I – I've hurt my ankle.'

I limp out of the shop and halfway down Hartington Drive, just in case she's watching.

Things get better. We eat two bowls of cornflakes each and write lists, planning what we have to buy to make this dump into a home.

'It's got potential,' Mum says.

'It's got mould in the bathroom,' I remind her.

'It's got fashionable, stripped-pine floor-boards . . .'

'With built-in creaks and woodworm!'

All three of us collapse in fits of giggles. OK, so it's not like we have much to laugh about, but it makes us feel better.

Our gloomy basement flat has two small, damp bedrooms, a large damp living room, an ice-cold, mouldy bathroom and a long, narrow kitchen with mustard-coloured walls and brown lino full of ciggy burns. It's dark, even in the daylight, because the windows are high up and on a level with the ground outside. If we watch out for long enough, we'd probably see Mrs Green's feet in tartan slippers with pom-pom trim, shuffling past up there on the gravel. We're like hobbits, moles, rabbits.

We've gone underground.

We are the proud new owners (renters?) of two brown easy chairs, a three-bar electric fire with fake coal and dirty chrome trimmings, one soggy double bed (Misti and me), one dry single bed (Mum), a wardrobe with no door and a rickety table with four wooden chairs that don't match. In the kitchen there's a greasy old cooker, a stained enamel sink with a tap that drips and a swirly Formica worktop with four built-in cupboards underneath.

We have a beanbag, a pushchair and a dozen bin bags full of clothes, shoes, books, toys, CDs, saucepans, dishes and assorted junk. It's going to take more than that to make the transformation.

'Today,' Mum says, 'is a rainy day. Quite possibly the rainiest day we've ever been up against.'

I frown. It was dry half an hour ago, when I skulked down the road for milk and Smarties. Cold, but dry.

'Luckily,' Mum pushes on, 'I've been saving. Saving for a rainy day.'

So we pull on our coats and hats, we strap Misti into her pushchair, stuff in a few soft toys to keep her happy and head off for town.

I feed Misti Smarties, one by one, making her name the colours while Mum queues up in the bank and makes a cash withdrawal.

'One hundred quid, cash,' she whispers when we get outside. I whistle under my breath, impressed, and Misti scoffs another Smartie.

'It sounds like a lot, but we have to be careful . . . it won't go far. It took me months to save this, stashing odd pounds and pennies away. Once it's gone, that's that – we have to spend it wisely.'

Mum takes us to a carpet warehouse and buys a vast offcut of speckly blue carpet for £25. It's thin and nylon and scratchy, but it's also big, cheap and blue. Blue is Mum's lucky colour, so there's no way we're about to complain.

The carpet is too big to carry, but the bloke in the shop winks at Mum and says he's got a delivery later near Hartington Drive, and he'll drop it off, no problem, no extra charge.

In a side street, just behind the sports centre, Mum discovers a junk shop selling a chest of drawers and a wide, wobbly bookcase for £10 apiece. For an extra £2, the lady will arrange to get them delivered.

They're seriously grim, but Mum promises she can make them cool and gorgeous.

We go to a shop that sells wallpaper, and Mum finds loads of little tins of paint in a big basket, reduced to 50p each. We pick every colour we can stand the sight of, then Mum splashes out on a huge tin of emulsion in cornflower blue.

'Kitchen,' she says, grinning. 'Bathroom too, if there's enough left over. Ooh, we'll need a roller . . .'

We grab a packet of cheap brushes, because the rollers are too pricey, and Mum hands over £16 for the lot.

Next we go food shopping. We trudge to a funny supermarket just out of the town centre where the tins and packets are stacked up on the floor instead of on shelves. You can buy twelve tins of baked beans for a quid.

We stock up on beans, pasta, peanut butter and cereal like we're expecting some kind of siege. Then we add washing powder, soap, shampoo, Marmite, cheese, milk, bread, bananas.

Misti's asleep by the time we're on to the cleaning gear, cruising the aisles of a cut-price hardware store, grabbing bleach, washing-up liquid, candles, scourers.

I've glazed over, bored, tired. I think about what I'm missing at school. Games this afternoon, maybe netball, loping about the playground trying to avoid the ball and Miss McDougall's sharp tongue at the same time.

I wonder if Jo's missing me. Is she sorry she was

so moody yesterday? Does she believe me now? Or is she hanging out with Aisha Patel, slagging me off and asking Aisha over to play after school?

I scowl horribly to stop myself from getting sniffly.

Mum remembers the powercards and sprints off to stock up on a few so we'll have light, heat and a hot meal later. My arms are aching from the heavy bags and I'm sick to death of shopping, walking and trying to get excited about a damp, greasy cellar in a tatty, crumbling old wreck of a house.

I push Misti over to a bench and sit down wearily, avoiding the chewing gum. It's starting to drizzle, so it looks like Mum has her rainy day after all.

She comes up behind me and we're huddled together before I know it, snuggled up like ragamuffin gypsies in the rain.

'You must be tired, Indie. I know I am. Starving too. And poor old Misti – she's been an angel. God, you don't deserve this.'

I frown hard and wipe my face. It's just the rain, honest. Mum doesn't deserve this either. Not the bruises, not any of it.

'Hey!'

Mum's on her feet, waving a £20 note in the air and ploughing through the crowd with the pushchair. 'Look at us – faces like a wet weekend! We're hungry, we need cheering up – how about Pizzaland, one last blowout? What d'you say?'

'Yes! Yes, please . . . oh, yes!'

7

It's not finished exactly, but it's a whole lot better.

We have scrubbed the floors, washed the walls, wiped the grime and mould off doors, windows and skirting boards. We have scoured the grease from the kitchen tiles and doused the cooker, the bath and the loo in bleach cleaner. For days, all I could smell was bleach.

Now all I can smell is paint. We painted the kitchen walls cornflower blue – Misti did the low-down bits, I did the middle bits, and Mum stood on chairs and worktops to reach the high bits. We worked on a different wall each and moved round, so as not to drip paint all over each other. We still got speckled with blue. Blue fingers, blue splattered clothes, blue freckled faces, blue streaks in our hair.

Misti had stiff blue palms, cornflower-coloured face-paint and a solid blue fringe. We decided the blue footprints she'd made across the ratty old lino could stay.

When we'd finished we had bubble baths to soak off all the stains and streaks and blobs, then flopped down in the brown easy chairs and toasted our toes with the three-bar electric fire going full blast.

Misti and I fell asleep curled up, and when we woke Mum was painting the bathroom blue too. It was three in the morning. The fire was still blazing, the lights were still on and Mum's favourite Oasis CD was playing quietly on my totsy CD player. It felt safe and warm, so I wriggled around a bit and went back to sleep.

We've been here five days now, and the flat is no longer brown and dark and cold.

The new carpet, not as scratchy as I thought, almost fits the room, and the floorboards that still show have been painted cornflower blue. The wet mattress is scrubbed and dry, and carefully disguised with a rumpled duvet and a scattering of soft toys.

The bookcase is rainbow-striped now, and loaded with paperbacks, board games and little baskets, boxes and bundles of pencils, brushes, scissors, beads, threads, wools and stacks of coloured card and paper. Misti has already produced a pasta/sequin/tinsel collage, pinned in pride of place above the leccy fire.

The doorless wardrobe is stuffed with freshly ironed clothes, the squeaky chest of drawers is scarily polka-dotted and packed with knickers, socks, tights, T-shirts.

Misti's dolls are scattered across the carpet in a way they never were at Max's, and it's spaghetti for tea.

When the doorbell rings – thin and reedy and unfamiliar – we all jump. Then Mum laughs and says it's only Jane, and I run to open the door.

Jane is Mum's friend. They've known each other since we first moved here from Wales – she's just about the only friend Max hasn't stopped Mum from seeing. He tried, I think, but Jane is too sensible and determined to let herself be sidelined.

Jane works in an office and wears perfectly pressed suits in navy, grey or black with T-shirts or polo-neck sweaters in pale pastel shades. She wears high-heeled shoes that click when she walks and her hair is cut into a short, layered bob with expensive chestnut streaks among the mousy brown.

It's just the turquoise and silver dangly earrings and bracelet and the small tattoo on her shoulder blade (only visible when swimming – Jane doesn't do skimpy clothes) that betray the fact she's not as sensible as she seems. Jane and Mum can talk for hours about dodgy music from the dim and distant past, about men, fate, reincarnation and whether feng shui, aromatherapy or meditation can save the world. Flaky. Seriously.

'Wow,' Jane says, stepping inside and looking around. 'How long have you been in? Five days? What a difference!'

Mum rang Jane and told her we'd moved, the day of our mega shopping trip and the Pizza-land blowout. Jane was round an hour later with a bunch of flowers, a bottle of wine and a card that said 'Good Luck in Your New Home' above a picture of the roses-round-the-door cottage I'd dreamed about that last day at school, waiting for Mum and Misti.

The night after, she appeared with an Indian takeaway, a big box of jelly babies and a vast, faded pink and sky-blue carpet that she claimed she was throwing out. (We put it down in the bedroom Misti and I share.)

Now she's coming to tea, for our official house-warming, and she's brought chocolate cake, lemonade, more wine and a bin bag full of curtains in midnight-blue velvet that she swears were going cheap in a charity shop.

We scoff spaghetti and cake and drink too much lemonade, and talk and laugh and turn the CD player up as loud as it can go so we can dance.

Misti crashes out on the brown squashy chair, cake crumbs all round her mouth, and Mum lifts her gently and carries her to bed, tucking her in with the old pink rabbit whose ears she loves to chew.

Then Mum and Jane crack open the wine and start talking grown-up stuff, so I stretch out on my beanbag with a sketchbook and a bundle of felt pens.

I draw the dream cottage with roses round the door, a mum and two little girls skipping through gardens that are filled with flowers. I draw a rainbow, a crock of gold and lots of green, rolling hills, more like the ones near Gran's house in Wales than anything in our grimy northern town.

I draw a doodle in the corner that looks suspiciously like Max, then scrawl a big cross right through the middle to show he's not wanted here. That makes me feel guilty, because it's not like Max ever did anything mean to me. He could be good fun sometimes, bringing home pocketfuls of penny sweets and giving me two quid every Saturday to wash the big blue builder's van. It looks like he's history now, though.

I yawn and lie down for a while, and when I wake, stretching lazily and pushing felt pens across the carpet, Mum is crying quietly into her wine and Jane is handing her tissues and patting her hair.

'He's a loser,' Jane says gently. 'He'll never change, Anna, you *know* that.'

'I know, I know . . .'

'You're better off without him. Look at you all, you can *breathe* here – you're not all creeping around scared to make a noise, say the wrong thing.'

'I know,' Mum sobs. 'It's just . . .'

'Just what?' Jane wants to know.

Mum pushes a curtain of fair hair back from her tear-stained face and smiles sadly. 'Oh, Jane,' she says. 'I know you're right, I *know*. It's just that – well, I still love him. I can't help it.'

8

Mum writes me a note to say I've had a bad cold and packs me off to school. I'm glad to escape the smell of paint and the wimpy electric fire and the big double bed that still smells faintly of pee. I have been dreaming of spelling tests and the nine times table and school stew for five days, but I feel oddly nervous as I mooch through the streets.

I'm not early – not early enough, anyway.

Getting lost in the graffiti-walled estate doesn't help. I walk around for ages through rabbit-warren streets that look identical, my feet crunching on glass. A gang of small boys follow me for a while, shouting rude things about my blue fleece bobble hat, but I blank them and they melt away, bored. In the end, I emerge somewhere near the chippy, which means I've trudged right round in a circle. I have to skirt round the estate, instead, sulking furiously.

The bell is ringing as I slip through the gates,

and long jaggedy lines of kids swarm around the doors, pushing and shoving to get inside. It's taken me a *whole hour* to walk here, all because Hartington Drive is in the back of beyond.

I'm last through the classroom door, and Miss McDougall clocks me as I try to sneak invisibly to my seat.

'Ah, Indigo,' she booms, so that just about every head in the room swivels to stare. 'Everything all right? How is your grandmother?'

'Um, fine, I think . . .'

'Do you have a note? Did you remember your topic homework?'

I give her the letter, return the emergency bus fare from last week and mumble something about dropping my topic book in a puddle, which doesn't go down too well. Then Miss McDougall turns her attention to Shane Taggart, who makes a late but spectacular entrance on his skateboard, school bag flying out behind him. He gets a hundred lines for his trouble.

I edge along to my desk, then stop, the colour draining from my face. Aisha Patel is sitting in it, and she and Jo are so busy chatting and laughing they don't even see me turn from white to pink to deep, dark red.

'Had a brilliant time . . . your mum's so nice . . . swimming club was excellent . . . do you think it's too late for me to start gymnastics? My mum and your dad could take turns with the driving . . .'

I shuffle past and park my stuff at Aisha's desk, because I know that if I say anything to her or Jo right now I'll live to regret it. And Aisha Patel might *not* live to regret it.

I sit down, feeling sick and shaky. I make a big deal out of rummaging in my bag, because I'm scared that I might cry, and there's no way I want anyone to see.

'Hey, Indie, you're back! How's your gran? Is she OK?'

Why the sudden interest in Gran?

Aisha is fussing round my desk (her desk), beaming and telling me how much everyone's missed me, how they were all so worried in case I'd gone forever.

'What exactly are you talking about?'

Aisha says it's OK, they all know, because Kevin Parker's dad met Max in the Fox and Squirrel a few days back, and Max told him we'd gone down to Wales because Gran was ill.

'He thought you'd be away quite a while,' Aisha gushes, all sympathy and concern.

'Well, I'm not,' I say coldly. 'I'm back. And, yeah, I can *see* you've missed me.'

Aisha looks crushed, and for a moment I feel bad, like I've stepped on her pet hamster or something. Then I remember. She's the one who's pushed me out of my seat. She's the one who's stealing my best friend.

'I'll get my stuff,' Aisha says in a small, hurt voice, and I want to slap her for being so weak, so wimpy. If she were tough and mean and spiteful, she'd be easier to hate.

Still, I'm doing my best.

She scoops up her books and her bag and we swap seats. Jo pinches me hard as I flop down, and I giggle and swat her back and I can breathe again, because somehow, at last, everything is going to be OK.

'So ... how was Wales?' Jo whispers later as we plough through a shedload of fractions. Miss McDougall can be really spiteful on a Monday morning.

'Wales?'

'You know, your gran, all that stuff. I don't suppose you had time for postcards.'

'Jo, we didn't *go* to Wales,' I tell her. 'My gran's fine. Really. That was just some line Max gave out to Kevin Parker's dad.'

'Why would he do that?' Jo puzzles.

I shrug.

'Embarrassed?' I suggest.

'About what?'

I look at Jo. She really hasn't a clue what's been happening in my life over the last few days.

'I *told* you we were moving,' I say, inventing some creative fraction answers for Miss McDougall to mark wrong.

'But Kevin Parker said that Max said . . .'

I make a huffy noise, put down my pencil.

'Mum's left Max.'

Jo whistles under her breath, and I can see, at last, I've got her attention.

'I didn't think . . . you've really moved?'

'To the mouldy basement from hell.'

Miss McDougall cruises noiselessy to a halt beside our desk and clears her throat in a talk-any-more-and-you're-dead kind of way.

I huddle down over my fractions, scrawl in a few more imaginary answers and doodle hearts and flowers and crescent moons all down the margins.

At break, we lie in the grass at the edge of the sports field and paint our nails with purple glittery nail varnish from Jo's stash.

'Why did your mum leave Max?' Jo wants to know. 'Is he having an affair? Is she?'

'*No!* Course not,' I say indignantly. 'I think . . . I don't know. Max was grumpy all the time. Mum just got fed up.'

'Fed up?'

Jo's not convinced. She wants drama, passion, soap-opera details.

She's not going to get them, though. I need to get my head round what's happened. I need to get so I don't feel scared and ashamed and confused every time I think about it.

'They were just rowing all the time. It wasn't working.'

'They fell out of love . . .' Jo sighs.

Like I told you, she reads too many slushy magazines.

I open the silver nail varnish and blob tiny silver spots on her perfectly painted nails.

'Yeuchh! How am I going to eat my crisps *now*?' Jo demands.

'With great difficulty,' I grin, tearing open the packet and feeding her a large sliver of cheese and onion.

'Pig,' she says. 'I missed you.'

'Missed you too.'

It's not warm exactly, but we grin and stretch ourselves out in the watery April sunshine. School's not so bad, if you don't count the lessons bit.

'Will we do our toenails too?'

'OK. Silver with crisp-crumb sprinkles?' Jo suggests.

We take off our shoes and socks.

'Is it really the flat from hell?' she asks, and I tell her all about 33 Hartington Drive with its hot and cold running damp, the brown lino with blue Misti-footprints all over it, the grim landlady who looks like she's about a hundred and three.

I tell her how we cleaned the whole place from top to bottom, then decorated till every surface was bright and fresh and clean. I tell her about the bookshelf with the multi-coloured stripes, the polka-dotted drawers.

'Sounds cool,' Jo says. 'Can I come over? See your new room? I'll bring my CDs . . .'

'Probably. I'll ask my mum.'

We paint our toenails silver with big purple spots, and when the bell goes we have to limp across the playground barefoot because the varnish is still wet. Miss McDougall marches down the line, sniffs loudly when she sees our feet and confiscates the nail varnish till home time. Then she makes us put our socks and shoes back on, so we both get smudgy toes.

Later, we're eating lunch and giggling, when I see Aisha hovering at a distance, looking at us wistfully. You can tell she'd love to come and giggle too, but she's not sure. Not sure if she's welcome.

I flash her a fake, cheesy smile, a told-you-so grin, and she starts smiling back before she twigs I'm not being friendly. Her face falls, and she takes her tray over to a table where Miss McDougall is sitting with a couple of Year Five girls.

I feel kind of mean, but then Aisha's not really a friend or anything. She thinks that hanging around grinning a lot and trying to tag along can change that – bet she thought her luck had changed when

I was off school. All she had to do was move seats and she had a ready-made mate.

It's not like Jo is missing her, though. Not like she missed me.

Tough luck, Aisha.

10

At home time, Jo sprints off the minute the bell goes – she's got swimming class right after school. I dawdle through to the corridor, shrug on my fleece and then mooch back to the classroom for my bag.

'Got no home to go to, Indigo?' Miss McDougall asks brightly.

'Yes, Miss. Sorry, Miss.'

'Your cold's all better now, then?' she presses.

I nod, sniffing loudly for good measure.

'Well, anyway, I'm sorry I got the wrong idea about your gran being ill. That'll teach me to listen to Kevin Parker. And by the way, your mum called the office this morning about the change of address. I hope it'll be a happy home for you, Indigo. I hope things will be better now.'

I blush to the very roots of my hair. What does she mean? What does she know?

'If there's ever anything you want to talk about, Indigo . . .'

'Yes, Miss. No, Miss. I mean, there isn't. I have to go . . .'

Miss McDougall means well, but I think I prefer her when she's all tweedy and strict, dishing out lines and homework and confiscating nail varnish.

I slouch across the playground, and though I should be chirpy because Mum promised sausages for tea, I'm not. I hate this walk home. I hate the estate. I hate 33 Hartington Drive. I hate . . .

Max.

It's Max, over the road from the school, leaning against his van, smoking lazily. My heart thumps and I try to look away, walking faster.

'Hey, Indie!'

I look round, lost, and he's walking over, the ciggy chucked to the gutter, his face all smiles, his blue eyes sparkling like there's nothing wrong in the whole wide world.

'Indie, how's it going? Good to see you! I had a job just over the road, thought I'd just hang on and say hi . . .'

'Hi!' I try to stop my face from grinning, but fail. I'm pleased to see him. Scared but pleased. Sick but happy.

'So . . . how's your mum? Calmed down a bit, d'you think? I mean, Indie, it was just a row, you know, grown-up stuff. Nothing to make such a big deal of. No reason to go uprooting you and Misti . . .'

I'm still smiling, but I can remember the night of the row pretty clearly, and the morning after. I remember Mum's face. Nothing to make a big deal of.

'Look, Indie, pet, I *love* you and Misti. I love your mum. She's made her point, so why can't she just come home now? Why don't I give you a lift back to wherever you're staying, talk to her?'

Max reaches out to throw an arm round my shoulders, but I flinch away. Mum doesn't want to talk to him. Mum doesn't want to see him.

I don't want him to know where we live.

'Come on, Indie. We'll get chips on the way, surprise the girls . . .'

'*No!*'

Max takes a step back, still grinning, holding his hands out in surrender.

'Just an idea. Another time, maybe. Hey, just tell your mum you saw me, OK? Tell her I miss her. Tell her it's OK to come home. Will you do that for me?'

I nod, staring at my feet.

'Look, I've gotta go, Indie, but I'll see you again. It's OK, really. Just a silly row, nothing serious. We'll get it sorted out. Tell your mum.'

I give him a shaky wave and start walking. I feel sick, I feel bad, I feel scared.

What was I supposed to do? Ignore him? Take the lift?

What do I tell Mum?

I look back as I turn the corner, and Max is sitting at the wheel in his van, watching me. He waves as I tear my eyes away again.

Why didn't Mum tell me this might happen? Why didn't she tell me what to do? Will she be cross I didn't bring him home? We could have had lemonade and chips and Mum and Max could have talked things through, made it up. Max could have rescued us from damp walls and brown lino, taken us back home in the back of the blue builder's van.

Maybe. Maybe not.

Mum loves him, she said that the other night. But she doesn't want to live with him. She doesn't want him to know where we live, I know she doesn't.

I'm halfway round the dodgy estate before the bad feeling starts to fade. It's OK. Max had a job near the school, that's all. It wasn't like he was lying in wait for me. He was just being thoughtful. Mum won't be cross.

He wouldn't follow me, he *wouldn't*.

But when I look behind, there's a blue van, way,

way in the distance, parked in at the kerb. Too far away to see if it's Max. It *can't* be.

I start to hurry, walking fast, but when I reach the next corner and look back the same blue van is crawling closer.

I'm running then, faster than I ever would in any race, dodging between the cars, thumping along the pavement, hurtling round the corner into Hartington Drive.

I look back and there's no blue van, no Max, and I'm into the driveway of number 33, round to the back, down the steps and into the flat. I'm shaking and my breath comes in great gasping sobs that burn my lungs and throat.

My face is wet with tears.

11

Mum strokes my hair and hugs me tight, and tells me I did the right thing. She wipes my face with a tissue and makes me hot chocolate.

I let its sweetness seep through me, calming, warming. Mum sits across the table, drinking black coffee, and Misti sprawls on the carpet, unpacking my school bag and swishing books, papers and pens across the floor.

'Maybe you were wrong about the blue van,' Mum says. 'Could you have been wrong? It was far away, you said. Maybe it was a different van.'

'Maybe,' I say. But I know it wasn't.

'Max wouldn't follow you. He wouldn't want to scare you. He wouldn't want to hurt us.'

Her fingers stray to the faded bruises along her cheek and jaw.

'He says he loves us,' I tell her. 'He says it was just a silly row, and we can come back any time.'

'Yes, of course,' Mum says. 'But, Indie, it was

just one silly row too many. We're better off here, love. I'm sorry for what happened at the school, but you did right. You did right.'

And though it's not even five o'clock yet, she stands up and moves around the flat, pulling across the blue velvet curtains, shutting out the light. Shutting out Max.

'Mum . . .'

'Yes, love?'

'It's just . . . Max was going to give me a lift back. He was going to get chips for us all, come and see Misti, talk to you. What if I'd said yes?'

Mum takes in a deep breath. 'If you'd said yes . . . well, that would have been OK too,' she decides. 'We'd have coped. But I'm glad you didn't, Indie.'

'So am I.'

I finish my hot chocolate and try to change the subject. 'We're learning about the Victorians at school,' I tell Mum, who is staring blankly at her empty coffee mug. 'I've got to make a project book, work on it at home.'

'Mmmm.'

She's miles and miles away, her face all sad and anxious. It makes me nervous.

I spend a while drawing out an elaborate title page, with a lady in a big crinoline dress and *The Victorians* written out in big, old-fashioned letters.

I add my name at the bottom, then a border of daisies for good measure. I colour it in with pencil crayons, because Misti is using my felts to draw huge, psychedelic swirls all over her arms and legs.

I'm hungry, but Mum seems to have forgotten about tea. I raid the biscuit tin and find three crumbly fig rolls. I eat one, give one to Misti, one to Mum. It's kind of a hint.

Mum gets up abruptly, but even I can tell she's not thinking food. Misti grabs the abandoned fig roll.

Mum opens the door and starts up the steps in the dusk.

'Mum? What are you doing?'

She looks back at me, forehead creased. It's like it's taking an effort for her to see me at all.

'I just wanted to check that it wasn't Max's van . . . make sure he's not hanging around some-where, looking for us. I'll feel safer if I know he's not there.'

I'm frowning now. If Max *is* out there watching for us, looking for him isn't a brilliant plan. If Mum spots *him*, the chances are he'll spot her.

'Is that a good idea?' I ask.

Mum must think so, because she runs across the drive and into the street, her eyes searching up and down the road. I duck inside, grab Misti and bundle her outside, grizzling. We stand a few feet away from Mum, watching.

There is no blue builder's van. She stares into the distance for a long time, jumping every time a car turns the corner. In the end the light has gone, and she leans against one huge gatepost, looking sad, lost, alone.

I lean against the other, feeling worried. Misti is asleep on my shoulder, and my back is aching.

Mum jumps forward again as something scoots round the corner, engine slowing as the headlights get closer. For a moment, the sick, scared feeling is back, and then the headlights whirl round into the drive and I can see it's just a car, the smart red Fiat I've seen parked here before.

The Fiat parks neatly, the engine dies, the lights fade and a young bloke in a suit gets out, struggling with a briefcase, a newspaper and two bulging bags of shopping.

'Hello there . . . everything OK?' he says to his weird welcoming committee.

'Yeah, fine,' I mumble, dragging Misti round so she's resting on my other hip. 'We were just . . .'

Then Mum's at my side, and the sad, anxious look is gone from her face. She's OK again.

'Just looking out for someone,' Mum says, hauling Misti out of my arms and cuddling up to her. 'It doesn't matter. Sorry if we startled you.'

'No problem! You must be the new people in the basement flat,' he grins. 'I'm Ian Turner. I live in the attic flat. I think it was the servants' quarters once.'

He holds out a hand and we all shake it, dutifully, while Mum introduces us in turn.

'See you around, then,' he says, with a special smile at Mum. 'If you ever need to borrow a cup of sugar or whatever, come on up – I'm your man!'

'Thank you,' Mum says, smiling politely. 'I'll remember that. Come on now, girls, it's time to get indoors. It's turning chilly.'

We're down the steps and into the flat, and Mum's bustling about like nothing was ever wrong, switching on the leccy fire and rustling up emergency beans on toast for everyone. She glances at my project title page as she clears the table, and gives me a big thumbs up, so I know she approves.

'This house is Victorian, you know,' she tells me.

'It looks it,' I say. We both laugh.

Later, when Misti's asleep and I'm shuffling around in pyjamas, getting my gym kit sorted for tomorrow, I decide to get brave.

'Mum . . .'

She looks up from the sink where she's washing clothes by hand because the flat doesn't have a washing machine. 'Yes, pet?'

'Jo was asking . . . can she come over to tea one day? We could work on our projects together. I'd love to show her my new room.'

Mum frowns, and for a minute I think she's going to say no, but then she's smiling, telling me that's a great idea, why not, any day this week would be fine.

I can't wait to tell Jo. It's going to be great.

Miss McDougall has gone mad.

I mean, she *looks* quite normal (for her) and she sounds quite normal (a brisk tongue-lashing for Shane Taggart, who came to school wearing a red-spotted bandana tied gangsta-style round his head). But she's *not* normal, because instead of launching into spelling tests, mental arithmetic or ten laps round the running track to 'wake us up', she marches us through to the TV room and we squish into giggly rows on the carpet, wondering what delights await us.

Will it be a thrilling play, all in French, on the theme of camping, shopping or cooking a meal? Ah, *bon*. Will it be a yawn-inducing story set in a castle, where we have to remember the word for a medieval toilet or that criss-crossy thing that goes behind the drawbridge? (Portcullis. We had that programme last month.) Or will it be something scary and scientific, with jolly presenters in bootleg jeans and spiky hair trying to get excited about solids, liquids and gases? Who knows – who cares?

We shift about, trying to get comfy, and the programme starts.

This is the amazing bit: it's not French or history or science – it's some old film I once saw on TV on a rainy Sunday afternoon, all singing, dancing and drama. It's called *Oliver!*.

OK, it's old. It's probably not cool. It's sad and scary and funny and weird, but I love it, and I think the others do too, because there's no whispering, no shoving, no notes being passed. Shane Taggart doesn't fall asleep like he did in the castle programme. We're all watching, wide-eyed, because if nothing else, it has to be better than the literacy hour.

Way better.

By the time it's finished, we've missed playtime, but nobody complains at all.

Miss McDougall quizzes us on the video to prove we weren't asleep, but we're covered, no problem. Everyone knows the plot.

Oliver's this Victorian orphan boy who dares to ask for more gruel at the dingy workhouse where he lives. (Gruel is kind of like school dinner semolina, I think.) He gets chucked out for being cheeky and meets up with a whole bunch of pickpockets led by some old bearded guy called

Fagin. He has loads of adventures, makes friends with Artful Dodger and Nancy and runs into trouble with Bill Sykes, Nancy's no-good boyfriend. In the end, Bill kills Nancy (I saw Aisha wipe her eyes at this bit), Oliver gets reunited with his long-lost grandad and Fagin and Dodger just keep on picking pockets.

Oliver! is one of those mad old films where everyone keeps bursting into song the whole time, but it's not as cheesy as it sounds because the songs are either heart-tuggingly sad or really happy and fun.

Anyway, Miss McDougall asks if we'd like to learn some of the songs from the film, and everybody says they do. She has a stack of song sheets and a music tape, and next thing we know the whole class is belting out 'You've Gotta Pick a Pocket or Two' like our lives depend on it.

Miss McDougall gets Shane Taggart to be Dodger, Buzz Bielinski to be Fagin and Aisha Patel to be Oliver, with the rest of the class as the pickpocket gang. She produces a stash of brightly coloured silk squares for us to use as hankies and we launch into it again, this time with actions, a whole classfull of dodgy Victorian pickpockets, fleecing the rich of their multi-coloured hankies.

The bell goes for lunch, and there's a low groan of disappointment, a sound never before heard from Miss McDougall's class, at least not in living memory.

'Miss!' Shane Taggart calls out urgently.

'Yes, Shane?'

'Miss, why don't we do a play? Why don't we do a play of *Oliver!* for the whole school to see?'

The class erupts with squeaks of approval, suggestions of casting, volunteers to paint scenery, make costumes, sell tickets.

Miss McDougall stalks the aisles, gathering up silk squares and stuffing them into a bin bag. She reaches the front and faces us sternly.

'Silence!' she roars.

There's silence, except for someone's tummy rumbling in the row behind me.

'Class, I don't think you realize the amount of work involved in putting on a musical play. The singing practice, lines to learn, rehearsals. That's not to mention scenery, props, costumes, publicity . . . to try something this ambitious in less than four months . . .'

She shakes her head. 'I know it's your last year at Calder's Lane. It would be wonderful to go out with a bang, stage something special, but *Oliver!* . . . It's a very, very challenging piece. Are you prepared for the hard work and effort it would take?'

'Yes!'

We're all in it together, a great roar of agreement, a tidal wave of pleading and promise.

Miss McDougall holds her hand up and we subside into silence.

'In that case,' she says, 'I'm delighted. Let's do it!'

13

We're late, so it looks like we're getting the crusty bits from round the edges of the big, empty lasagne dishes, plus wilted salad and soggy tomatoes because the chips and veg are all gone. Miss McDougall sails to the head of the queue and smiles her sweet, friendly, no-nonsense smile. The dinner lady sighs and hauls out a vast, bubbling, brand-new dish of lasagne. Miss McDougall waits, holding her dish out, and eventually a tray of chips and a dish of green beans are produced.

The whole queue is grinning, saved from plates of cold, crusty leftovers.

Another stern look from Miss McD., and a new dish of treacle sponge with a jug of creamy yellow custard, strangely lump-free, appear.

'Bet they were saving that for themselves,' Jo whispers.

If Miss McDougall had been around a hundred

years ago, there'd never have been all that trouble about the gruel.

We crowd in at one of the few free tables, and for once I don't mind that Aisha Patel's squished in with us, because I can choose my moment and drop a few comments about Jo coming over if she tries to get too pally.

It's not a problem, though, because Shane, Buzz and Iqbal flop down in the three empty seats and all anyone can talk about is the play, Shane taking full credit for the fact that it's happening at all.

I have a sneaky idea Miss McDougall had it all planned out the whole time, but I don't want to spoil his moment of glory.

'I'm going to audition for Nancy,' Jo says, flicking her hair back and looking at Shane from underneath her eyelashes. 'It's the only really good girl's part, isn't it?'

'Bet you get it,' Aisha gushes. 'You're so pretty and confident. I mean, I'd be happy just to help behind the scenes . . .'

'Nah,' says Shane. 'You'll get a part, Aisha. You can sing, can't you? You have to be able to sing for a musical, it stands to reason.'

Jo looks faintly irritated. '*I* can sing,' she says.

Shane shrugs and dips a chip in his lasagne.

'You should audition for the star part, Shane,' Jo pushes. 'You'd make a great Oliver.'

'Nah, too wimpy. I'd rather be the Artful Dodger. That'd be a right laugh! Or Fagin. How about you, Indie?'

I pull a face and pretend I'm not that bothered, but the truth is I'd try out for any part, because I love drama. I spend my school days being told off for daydreaming, but being an actor . . . isn't that like daydreaming for a living? Trying on other people's lives to see how they fit?

Suddenly I can feel Shane looking at me, his green eyes searching my face, and my cheeks flame pink. He starts laughing and nicks a couple of my chips, but I know I didn't imagine it because Jo is staring at me, stony-faced, and Buzz and Iqbal are nudging each other and making leery 'way-hey-hey' noises.

'I'm not really interested,' I say to Jo helplessly. I mean the flirty looks, not the play, and I hope they all get the message. Jo still looks furious, though.

She offers Shane her chips, but Buzz and Iqbal scoff them instead, and by the time we get to the treacle pudding Shane has switched the conversation to skateboarding and they're rattling on about half pipes, ollies and grinders.

Jo makes one last attempt to get Shane's

attention. 'You're great on that skateboard,' she says. 'I'd love to have a try, but it just looks *so* difficult . . .'

This is the girl who can do a handstand on the balance beam and follow it off with a somersault before landing in the splits. She's been doing gymnastics since she was *four*.

I try to remember what her beloved teen mags say, and decide Jo's got hormone trouble. Growing up is a very scary thing. I hope it never happens to me.

Shane smiles, and tells her he'd be happy to give her lessons, any time.

'And you two, of course,' he adds, with a flash of grin to Aisha and me. Then he's away, Buzz and Iqbal following in his wake, and Jo's glaring at me.

'Did you *have* to keep butting in?' she explodes. 'That was a private conversation. It's *me* he likes, Indie, so why do you have to get in on the act? You're just so *childish* . . .'

'But I didn't . . .'

Jo's eyes flare. 'You *did*. Aisha saw, didn't you, Aish? Why can't you just back off?'

'But . . . Look, Jo, I'm sorry,' I manage. 'I didn't mean anything. I just didn't think . . .'

'Don't get all wound up,' Aisha pleads. 'He did say he'd give you lessons on the skateboard. He must like you. And we don't want to fall out over a lad . . .'

We?

But Jo softens. 'D'you think he really does fancy me?' she demands.

'Er, well, probably . . .' Aisha says.

'Definitely,' I add, wondering when I got to be such a good liar.

We finish our treacle sponge and listen to Jo telling us how she's been crazy about Shane Taggart since Year Two. I frown. Since last week, more like, but I'm not about to argue.

'I'm definitely trying out for the part of Nancy,' she says. 'Shane's bound to get a good part, and we'd be rehearsing together the whole time. He'll definitely notice me then.'

'Bound to,' Aisha echoes.

'Will you two help me learn my lines for the auditions?' Jo asks, giving us both her poor-lost-little-kitten look.

'No problem,' Aisha nods, and somehow that's the last straw. Shane makes me blush, Jo's hacked off with me and now Aisha's moving in on my best mate.

'We could run lines at my place one night after school,' I suggest, looking straight at Jo. 'I asked Mum and she said any night this week would be fine. What day suits you, Jo?'

Jo reels off her social diary. Swimming on Mondays, gymnastics tonight and Thursday, violin Friday . . . we decide on tomorrow, as long as Jo's mum agrees.

'We can listen to CDs and read mags and go through your lines for the audition . . .'

I'm keeping my eyes on Jo so I don't have to face Aisha. I don't want to see her disappointment, don't want to see her sad brown eyes or her trembly lips.

But Jo hasn't forgiven me, not quite.

'Is Wednesday OK for you too, Aisha?' she says. And she's smiling, because she wants to see if I have the guts to tell Aisha she can't come. She wants to see me squirm.

My face burns for the second time in half an hour, and I drag my rotten, lousy eyes up from the tabletop to meet Aisha's.

'I – I'm not sure – my mum didn't say about you, Aisha . . .'

I'm a liar, a worm, a coward.

'You see, we've only just moved in . . .'

Aisha looks like she's sorry for me, like I'm something to be pitied: a small, slimy slug that crawled in from the rain.

'I can't do Wednesday, anyhow,' she says. 'I'm busy.'

'Oh, well, that's a shame,' Jo gushes. 'Never

mind, though, another time, hey? *I'll* definitely be there, Indie. I'm looking forward to it.'

Great. That makes one of us, then.

14

'Sorry, Aisha,' I say yet again as Jo and I get our stuff together to walk home on Wednesday. 'Maybe another time?'

'Maybe.'

How come I feel so guilty? Possibly because Jo's been stirring it every chance she can get, till I'm almost wishing it *was* Aisha, not her, coming round for tea.

'You can come over to mine any time you like, Aisha,' Jo puts in, ever generous. '*My* mum's not funny about visitors.'

I have to bite my lip to stop the tears prickling at the back of my eyes. What is it with Jo? Is this all because Shane Taggart nicked my chips?

We wave bye to Aisha at the gates and turn up towards the estate.

'Is it far?' Jo wants to know. 'Is there a bus?'

I show her the money Mum gave me for bus fares, and we decide to spend it on sweets and walk instead. We buy ice pops and penny chews and strawberry laces, and Jo links my arm as we mooch along on a sugar high, telling me I'm her best, best mate.

Two weeks ago, I know I was. Our friendship was unshakeable, the kind that lasts forever. I could have pictured us sat side by side in the old folks' home, squirting each other with lavender water, painting each other's nails lime green and sharing strawberry laces and Ovaltine.

Now I'm not so sure.

And I'm not even sure any more whether it's Aisha's fault, or Shane's or anyone else's fault at all. It's just me and Jo.

'Friends forever?' Jo squeezes my arm.

'Forever,' I say, knowing it's a wish and not a promise.

'Good. Aisha's just my second-best mate, OK? You're not to be jealous.'

What do you say to that?

By the time we reach the top of Hartington Drive, Jo's moaning that her feet hurt. 'It's stupid to move so far away from Calder's Lane,' she sulks. 'It's not even on a proper bus route, it takes ages to walk and it's all gloomy and tatty round here . . .'

'It's not like we had much choice,' I remind her.

'No, but . . . I mean, I'm surprised you're still going to our school. You must be well out of the catchment area. My cousin's mate lives near here, and he went to Templars Primary, then Rathbone High. I expect you'll have to go there.'

'No, I won't!'

Jo fixes me with a look. 'It's not up to you, is it?' she shrugs. 'It's up to the council. It's all about catchment areas and where you live. You can't just *choose.*'

'I'm going to Kellway Comp like everyone else,' I say, and I know that if Jo doesn't shut up about this I'm going to cry, or slap her, or both.

'We'll see,' she says, and we turn into the drive-way of number 33 just as Ian Turner is getting out of his red Fiat, bags and papers flapping as usual.

'Hello, Indie,' he says. 'Hello, Indie's friend.'

'Hello, Mr Turner.'

We clatter down the steps and into the flat.

'*He's* pretty lush,' Jo whispers. 'Too old for us, but I bet your mum fancies him . . .'

'She does not!'

The idea is so loopy it has me laughing again.

'They could get married!' Jo suggests. 'We could be bridesmaids!'

'In pink and lilac frocks with frills and big bows in our hair!'

Mum comes through from the bedroom carrying Misti, who's obviously been bathed and dressed in her best stuff specially.

'What's the joke?' she asks, and we collapse in giggles again, but Mum doesn't mind. She's got orange juice and chocolate chip cookies and Hula Hoops all set out on the table.

I love my mum.

We scoff the snacks and go through to my room, and it's all neat and tidy and smelling of joss sticks to disguise any lingering whiff of Misti-accidents. Jo admires the wardrobe, the spotty drawers and the turquoise fun-fur cushions my mum found in last year's Homebase sale. She chooses a CD and we turn up the volume and stretch out on the bed, doing flow charts and quizzes from a couple of teen mags Jo's brought along.

We discover that my perfect party snack is popcorn, and Jo's is peanuts; my dream date is a day at the ice rink, and Jo's is a candlelit dinner for two; my feel-good fashion is sassy skateboard chic and Jo's is glitz 'n' glam, all high heels, crushed velvet and dangly earrings.

We clean off Monday's nail varnish and repaint it, using 'Tangerine Dream' for me and 'Purple Passion' for Jo. No spots, no smudges, no crushed-crisp sprinkles. We even paint three of Misti's dinky little fingernails before she gets bored and wanders off to dunk all her soft toys in the bath-room sink.

'Teatime, girls,' Mum shouts through, and we

wolf down sausage, beans and mash. Mum says there's ice cream for afters.

'What kind?' Jo wants to know. 'My fave is that Häagen-Dazs one with the triple chocolate swirls . . .'

We've got economy vanilla from the cheap supermarket, but Mum lets us crumble a couple of choc chip cookies on top, and Jo says it's almost as good.

Afterwards, we go through our lines for the audition. Miss McDougall's given everyone the same chunk of script, because she says she's just looking for expression and confidence and potential. We're to get into groups and each read a character from the two-page test script, and Miss McDougall will make a shortlist and do the casting from that.

And Shane was right – we have to sing. Everyone who's trying out for a part has to do the pickpocket song, solo, in front of the whole class.

Jo reads Nancy, I read Oliver, and we leave out the bits for Dodger because Aisha's going to do that. Jo reads her lines really clearly, like she's reading out in assembly, or doing a talk in front of the class. Aisha's right: she's pretty, she's confident. She'll make a great Nancy.

'Do we do the singy bit too?' I ask, and Jo's away, wiggling her hips, whipping imaginary silk squares out of nowhere. She looks so convincing, you don't really notice the bits where her voice goes wobbly.

She flops back down on the bed. 'I *have* to get this part,' she says. 'It's perfect for me, isn't it? And I just know Shane's going to be Oliver or Dodger or something. I really want him to notice me, Indie. If I get the part, we'll have to practise together loads, and maybe he'll ask me out or something.'

I stare at Jo. Nobody in our class has ever been out with a boy, except for Carrie Naughton who says she had a holiday romance last summer and showed us a blurry photo of a geeky French kid as proof. And Kelly Murphy, who hangs out with Buzz Bielinski sometimes and says he once kissed her outside the chippy.

'D'you think he will?' Jo demands. 'Ask me out, I mean?'

'Probably,' I say. 'You're the prettiest girl in the class.'

'D'you think so? Does *he* think so?'

Jo looks so sad that I want to stroke her hair and tell her to forget about Shane Taggart cos he's just a sandy-haired, skateboard-mad, chip-stealing chancer. There's no way he's worth all the heart-ache, the hassle.

'Anyway,' Jo says, 'I fancied him first, so you

have to back off. I'd never forgive you if you went out with him, Indie. Never.'

'But I wouldn't – I don't even like him, not that way –'

I'm so shocked at the unfairness of it all, I'd laugh if Jo wasn't so serious.

'Just remember,' she says. 'Back off.'

We run some more lines and Jo tears out two posters from her magazines and says I can have them for my walls, and then Mum calls through because it's half seven and Jo's dad's here.

She's going.

I wish she'd never come here in the first place.

15

I'm sitting on the wall at school, eating a strawberry lace leftover from last night and wishing I could rewind my life and start again.

Mum's left Max, and I miss him, in a funny kind of a way. He shouted a lot and there were way too many rows, but he could be good fun too. And now it's over, and we're alone again.

Mum says she's strong, that she's come through worse than this, but I'm not convinced.

It'd be OK if only Jo wasn't losing the plot over Shane Taggart. It's crazy and irrational and it doesn't make any sense, so I know it has to be a growing-up thing and the way to go is to blank it, big style, and hope it goes away. It's not that easy, though.

'Hiya.'

I look up, and guess what, it's problem number three, Aisha, hovering a few feet away, smiling sadly and waiting for me to send her get-lost signals.

Somehow, this morning, I can't be bothered.

'Hi, Aisha.'

'How'd it go last night?'

'Oh, y'know. It was OK. We played CDs and did a whole bunch of quizzes from Jo's mags, and we went through our lines and stuff.'

'Sounds cool.'

Aisha gets brave and sits down next to me on the wall.

'Yeah, it was.'

'But . . .?'

'Oh, I dunno. Jo's hacked off with me cos she thinks I like Shane. I *don't*. D'you think I could be bothered to go chasing after some lad when everything's so . . . messed up? Well, anyway, I just don't, OK?'

I break off a length of strawberry lace and hand it over.

'Thanks.' Aisha chews thoughtfully. 'He likes *you*, though.'

'Did I ask him to?'

'No-o. It's just hard for Jo, that's all.'

'Look, it's hard for me too,' I say. 'I have enough problems without Jo going all funny on me. I've been best mates with her since we were in Reception class. Then, lately, everything's been going pear-shaped.'

Aisha looks away, biting her lip.

'Do you think it's my fault, some of this?' she asks in a tiny voice.

'Ten out of ten,' I say.

There's a long, long silence. I kick the gravel around at my feet and feel mean, but Aisha isn't stupid. She must know how I feel about her.

'It's not been a great year for me either,' she says eventually. 'Moving here, starting a new school in the middle of term. I know you and Jo aren't exactly over the moon to have me hanging around, but ... I had to try. I like you, both of you. I just wanted a chance.'

I scuff my shoes some more, feeling spiteful and selfish. I try, just as an experiment, to see things from Aisha's point of view.

'I'm not trying to steal Jo from you,' she says.

'No?'

'No. I promise. I didn't mean to stir things up. If you want me to get lost, I will.'

I look at Aisha and she tries to smile. I do too. Neither of us do very well.

The bell rings.

'So ...' Aisha says.

'So ... I dunno, Aisha. Maybe I'll just get used to you.'

'Maybe you will.'

Maybe pigs will fly.

*

When I get home, Misti's crying and Mum's got that creased, anxious expression again, like the day she stressed out thinking Max had followed me home. I chuck down my bag and give Misti a cuddle.

'Aw, she's all wet, Mum,' I say, wrinkling my nose. 'That's why she's crying.'

'Hmm?'

So I change Misti's nappy and wipe her legs with a flannel, dry them off and drag on clean tights. She's still grizzly, though.

'What's up, poppet? Want a biscuit?'

There's nothing left in the biscuit tin, so I make a peanut butter sandwich and Misti wolfs it down.

'Did you have any lunch?' I ask Mum, frowning.

'Lunch? Oh, no. I wasn't hungry.'

I look around. The blue carpet hasn't been hoovered, the bathroom's flooded from one of Misti's doll-washing games, the sink is full of last night's washing up.

'Mum, are you feeling OK?'

'What? Oh, yes, I'm fine. Is it teatime? Do you want something to eat?'

We make macaroni because there's loads of dried pasta on the shelf, but there's no milk or cheese so we can't have sauce. Mum opens a tin of tomatoes instead. It tastes pretty boring, but we eat it anyway. Then Mum curls up in one of the grotty brown chairs and her face goes all sad and closed again.

I tie a tea towel round Misti's waist and stand her on a kitchen chair, and we wash up. Misti sloshes the water around and makes mountains of bubbles, whooping and squealing, and I chip away at yesterday's frying pan with a wedge of scourer, then attack the pasta pan and the stack of plates.

I try teaching Misti the pickpocket song, and after a while we're belting it out full blast as we scrub and rinse and dry. I have to swab the kitchen floor with a used bath towel, to soak up the floods, then I move on and do the same in the bathroom, hauling a dozen badly mauled teddies out of the bath and lining them up near the leccy fire to dry.

Misti's soaked again by then, but at least it's only washing-up water this time. I change her nappy again and put her into her jammies. She's squealing for a story, so I read *Sleeping Beauty* from the big book of fairy tales, and before I get to the handsome prince part she's fast asleep, her fair hair spread out across the pillow.

'OK, Mum?' I ask as I come back through, but she's definitely not OK. 'Want to help me with my lines? It's the audition tomorrow.'

She doesn't even hear me.

'Mum, are you feeling ill? D'you need a herb tea or an aspirin or something?'

She shakes her head, and though it's hard to tell in this light because of the blue scarf draped over the standard lamp, I think she's been crying.

'*Mum?* Shall I get someone? The landlady, or Mr Turner from upstairs?' My voice is all wobbly and frightened now. I know something's wrong, but I don't know what to do.

'Mum, I'm going to ring Jane. Or Gran. Have you got some change? Where's the address book?'

I'm flicking through the blue velvet notebook when Mum gets to her feet, raking a hand through her tangled hair.

'Indie . . . look, I'm sorry. I'm OK, really. It's just – I had a bit of a shock today. I was going to the park with Misti when I saw Max's van. It just scared me. Silly, really. It was probably just coincidence.'

I bite my lip. 'Did he see you?'

'No. No, I don't think so.'

'I still think we should ring Jane. She'll know what to do.'

Mum pulls her jacket on, dredges the pockets for change. 'I'll do it, love, you stay here with Misti. I won't be long.'

She slips out of the door and I'm alone in the flat. It feels very empty, very silent. The leccy fire makes a clicking sound; the floorboards creak as I creep to the bedroom door to check Misti's still sleeping. The phone box is down on the corner, near the shop. Mum won't be long.

I look at my watch. Two minutes.

Why can't we have a phone here? I know the answer to that. No money, not till Mum gets herself a part-time job. Why can't we have a mobile? Same reason, plus Mum has this theory they're bad for you.

If you ask me, hanging around in a dingy basement flat with creaking floorboards and a clicking fire is bad for you too. Six minutes. She'll be there now. Hope it's empty, that she doesn't have to wait.

I sit down in the brown armchair. Maybe the fire is clicking because the powercard is running out. The lights seem to flicker. *Hurry up!*

Eleven minutes. There must be a queue. This was a bad idea, like pretty much every idea I've had lately. Twelve minutes.

I hunt around, looking for where Mum keeps the spare powercard. Not in the kitchen drawer, not on the bookcase. Not in her blue suede handbag, where there's a picture of me and Misti and Max, taken at Christmas. We all look so happy. We *were* happy, that day.

Twenty minutes.

It hits me.

Max. Max is out there, and he's seen her.

Maybe she's had to run, hide, duck down a side street. Maybe Max has caught her, and they're talking, shouting, fighting.

Maybe . . .

'OK, love?'

I look at my watch. Mum's been gone nearly half an hour, and I'm so glad she's back I fling myself into her arms, shaking.

'Mum, I thought . . .'

'Hey, hey, hey, Indie. It's OK. It's OK. I'm sorry I was so long.'

'Did you call Jane? Is she coming over?'

Mum frowns as she shrugs off her jacket.

'Jane? No, I didn't ring Jane. I rang *Max*. And it's OK, Indie, because he's *not* mad at us and he's *not* following us or anything. It was just a co-incidence, like I said. He understands that we need some space if we're going to work this thing out. It's OK, Indie. *Everything* will be OK now.'

16

We're out of breakfast cereal and milk, but Mum's still sleeping and I don't want to wake her. I make a jam sandwich instead.

It's audition day.

At school, everyone is talking about the play and Buzz Bielinski sits with a straight face and a false white beard right through registration, so it's not hard to guess he's hoping to be Fagin.

Jo is even scarier, with her hair all piled up into a bun, a ton of slides and loads of curly tendrils all round her ears and neck. She's tried out every make-up tip the teen mags have to offer – two-tone clashing eyeshadow, blusher, lipgloss and half a tub of body glitter in a vaguely cheekbone-like location.

'What's with the make-up?' I whisper while Miss McDougall sorts out the school dinner numbers.

Jo looks cross. 'Du-ur,' she says. 'Actresses *have* to wear make-up, don't they, because of all the stage lights? Besides, I want to attract Miss McDougall's attention.'

She's done that all right, judging by the withering glances she's getting. Buzz, Shane and Iqbal are looking too, and there's a whole load of giggling coming from their corner. Jo sends them a few flirty glances, subtle as a flying brick.

Thoughtful as ever, Miss McDougall has devised an *Oliver!*-themed spelling test to get us in the mood for the audition.

'Orphanage,' she says crisply, and everyone gets scribbling. 'Gruel.'

Then, gliding to a halt beside me and Jo, she adds in a whisper, 'Wash it off, Miss Ashton. *Now.*'

Jo turns crimson, which looks quite scary with the mauve and yellow eyeshadow and the glittery bits. But she doesn't argue. She stumbles to her feet and makes for the door.

'Pickpocket,' Miss McDougall booms out as the door clicks shut behind Jo. 'Punishment.'

We're lined up outside the hall, ready for the auditions, before Jo reappears. Her face is pink and scrubbed, her eyes red-rimmed and her lips set into a cold, thin line.

'She's a *cow*,' Jo hisses into my ear as Miss McDougall tells us to sit in our groups and read our lines until called to audition. 'I hate her.'

I squeeze her arm in sympathy.

The auditions are brilliant. Mr Lennon comes into the hall to help with the casting, and Kai's mum, who works part-time for the theatre in town, is there too. My tummy's all butterflies.

Melanie Curtis keeps getting her lines wrong, and she can't remember the words of the song. Buzz, Shane and Iqbal are so good that Carrie Naughton asks for their autographs. Kelly Murphy and her group have worked out a dance routine for the pickpocket song.

'Wish we'd thought of that,' Aisha says, but Jo's still fuming, scowling down at her script.

'Don't let her get to you,' I say. 'You'll be brilliant, I know you will.'

'Aisha Patel, Jo Ashton and Indigo Collins, are you ready?'

'Go, girl,' I whisper to Jo.

'I'll show her,' she says under her breath. And she does. Jo reads every line loud and clear. She doesn't stumble, she doesn't pause, and she even remembers to wave her arm around for emphasis like we agreed.

Miss McDougall nods, writing something down on a clipboard. She asks Aisha and me to read a chunk of script again, then it's time to sing, just one verse each, with Mr Lennon on piano to help with the tune. Aisha sings in a sad, clear voice, and I notice the other kids go quiet and watch. My turn. I imagine I'm Dodger, the cheeky pickpocket lad, singing, and put as much fun as I can into it all. I'm grinning all over my face as the piano dies away, and there's a couple of wolf whistles from the back of the hall that make Jo frown.

Her turn. She sings like she reads, loud and clear, but she's off-tune and her voice cracks and wobbles. I catch a glance between Miss McDougall and Mr Lennon, and I know it's not good news for Jo.

After lunch, Mr Lennon comes into class to announce the results. Buzz gets Fagin, Shane gets Dodger and Kai gets Bill Sykes. As Mr Lennon announces that Kelly Murphy gets the part of Nancy, I feel Jo stiffen in the seat beside me. I try to send her a not-fair look, but she's hiding her face in her hands. I hope she's not crying.

'Because it's such a tough part, we've decided to pick two actors to share the title role,' Mr Lennon says. 'We'll run the play for two nights, with a different Oliver on each.'

Iqbal? Kevin Parker? Who's left?

'Well done to our two stars, Aisha Patel and Indigo Collins . . .'

There's a roar of approval and more whistling and cheering from Shane's corner, and Aisha and I are looking at each other in shock, delight and horror. I want this part, I realize, more than I ever wanted anything. I want it so I can escape from damp basements and soggy little sisters and a mum who suddenly thinks it's a great idea to ring her ex and get chatting when we've all spent the last two weeks hiding from him.

Then I look at Jo, her face pale and her lip quivering, with hurt or with anger, I can't tell.

I don't want this part.

I want my best friend back, because I know, surer than anything I've ever known, that I've lost her. Maybe for good.

17

Mum's not well. She stays in bed all Saturday, curled up and crying, and I can't find any money for milk or bread or cheese or cereal. When I ask, Mum says she'll sort it, but she doesn't.

'Mu-um,' I say, and I can't help it if there's no sympathy or understanding in my voice. I can't help it if I sound hacked off and angry, because I am.

'We need *money*, Mum,' I say. 'Come on, there *has* to be some cash, somewhere. I need to buy stuff. Misti needs to eat. I need to eat. And if you're not going to talk to me, not going to look after us, then I need to ring Jane, because I'm *scared*.'

My voice has risen to a high-pitched, tantrum-style whine.

'*DO* something, Mum!' I scream. I want to chuck Mum's mug of stone-cold coffee across the flat. I want to shake her, slap her, wake her up.

My mum is sick and I'm shouting at her, scaring

her, scaring Misti. I'm a spoilt, selfish brat. I feel awful.

I sink down on the edge of the single bed, shaking. 'Sorry,' I whisper.

Mum just looks at me, her eyes wide, her lips quivering.

'Me too,' she says. Then she hugs me tight and the tears come again, making a wet patch on my top.

Misti and I play with play dough and teddies all day, and I heat a tin of tomato soup at lunchtime, but Mum won't eat any and Misti's still hungry. I can't ring Jane because I haven't any money, and it's too far to walk to her place, even if I knew the way from here. I'd have to take Misti and I'd have to leave Mum, and neither option sounds great.

In the end, I hear Ian Turner's red Fiat scrunch up the driveway and I run out and tell him Mum's not well, and ask if he has a phone I can use.

'Course you can,' Ian says, taking me up the steps to the big front door of number 33, across the dingy hallway that smells of polish and up the creaking staircase. 'There's a nasty flu bug going round at work. Loads of people off. Is that what's up with Anna?'

'Probably,' I say vaguely. 'I'm not sure.'

Ian's flat is tucked into the roof of the house, and though it's small, it's messy and bright and it doesn't smell of damp. He points to the phone and I dial Jane's number shakily.

She's there. Relief floods through me and I'm babbling about Mum being ill and Misti being hungry and Jane says she'll be with us in half an hour, hang on, keep smiling.

When I replace the receiver, Ian Turner comes out of the kitchen with a box packed with Lemsip, milk, cheese, bread, oranges, Jaffa Cakes and chocolate.

'Emergency rations,' he says, smiling, and even though I know Mum'll be cross, I let him follow me down the creaky stairs and round to the back.

Misti's sitting on the steps, wailing like her heart will break, and I scoop her up and breathe in her baby-powder smell and the scent of the cheap shampoo we're all using these days.

Inside, Mum is up, looking pale and sad and beautiful, her blue Chinese wrap tied round her, fair hair falling in limp corkscrew curls around her shoulders.

'Mr Turner . . . you really shouldn't have. You're very, very kind.'

She collapses into one of the brown armchairs and holds her arms out for Misti.

'No problem.' Ian Turner looks for the kettle, fills it and switches it on. He produces a Lemsip sachet and shakes the powder into a clean mug.

'Flu is a rotten thing, especially at this time of year. You have to just give in to it, I'm afraid.'

'I don't seem to have much choice . . .' Mum shrugs and leans back in the chair. Misti's quiet now, sitting on her lap, possibly because Ian's given her a Jaffa Cake.

'Jane's coming,' I say to Mum. 'I rang her.'

'I see,' Mum says. 'Well, help is at hand, Mr Turner. Thank you for everything, and don't worry, I'll replace the food as soon as I'm up and about . . .'

'No, no, I won't even miss it,' he says. 'Really, I don't eat much, living alone. If you like, I could stick around, fix you all a bite to eat . . .'

'No, thank you, Mr Turner. We'll be fine.'

'Ian,' he says. 'We're neighbours, after all.'

'Ian.'

He smiles and nods and backs away, letting himself out of the flat.

'Indie . . .' Mum starts, but I interrupt.

'I know, I know, but what was I supposed to do? No money, no food, and you just keep on crying . . . We're hungry, Mum. I had to ring Jane, and how *else* was I meant to do it? What d'you *expect*?'

Mum leans forward in the armchair, so that her hair screens her face. 'I don't know,' she whispers. 'I don't know . . .'

'Mum – look, just drink the medicine, OK?' I tell her. 'You'll feel better.'

'I won't,' she says into Misti's blonde curls. 'I won't, Indie, because it's not flu, and this won't cure it. Nothing will.'

The doorbell shrills, and Misti squirms free of Mum's hug and tumbles over to the door with me.

'Jane, Jane, Jane!' she squeals as I open the door and Jane bustles in, carrying a huge, flat box smelling gorgeously of pizza. We fall on the food like we haven't eaten for a week, except for Mum, who picks up a slice and stares at it like she's trying to identify an alien species.

'Hey, come on, Anna, you have to eat,' Jane says. She prods at the untouched Lemsip, still warm, and frowns. 'We have to get you better. This'll help.'

'It's not flu,' I say.

'Oh? What is it?'

A fat tear rolls down Mum's cheek.

Jane shoves her pizza to one side and grabs Misti's tartan blanket from the floor. She drapes it gently round Mum's shoulders and settles her back in the brown armchair, facing the fire.

'Come on, Anna, love, you know he's not worth it,' she says softly, and then Mum's sobbing, howling, drawing in big gulps of air. Misti looks up, stricken, and starts to cry too. My hands are shaking, and my mouth feels like sawdust.

'Early bedtime?' Jane suggests, holding Mum as her body shakes and shudders. 'Pizza in bed?'

'Hear that, Misti? Midnight feasts!' I pick her up and troop across to the bathroom, hushing and stroking her, telling her things are fine.

My acting skills just get better and better.

I wash her tomato-smeared face and change her nappy, and we shuffle through to the bedroom, then huddle up together in bed. I read her *Cinderella* from the big book of fairy tales, feeding her bites of pizza and cuddling her till she falls asleep.

Who's going to do that for me?

When I'm sure Misti won't wake, I slip out of bed and creep to the bedroom door.

Mum and Jane are curled up in the twin brown armchairs, nursing coffees in the pool of blue light from the lamp.

'Do you think that ringing him was a good idea?' Jane is saying quietly.

'Yes,' Mum says. 'I had to, didn't I, to warn him off? We can't make a fresh start with Max hanging around the whole time, trying to follow us, trying to find out where we live. I had to tell him to back off.'

'And did you?'

'Sort of,' Mum stares down into her coffee cup. 'Look, Jane, it's not like you think. He's a good man, really – why d'you think I stayed with him so long?'

Jane shakes her head.

'He wants to change, he wants to work it out,' Mum rushes on. 'And he misses the kids – he's Misti's dad, after all. I just don't know if I can trust him. Oh, Jane, he's got me so mixed up – I don't know *what* I want any more.'

'To be safe? To be happy?' Jane suggests.

Mum slumps forward, her head in her hands. 'But it's so hard,' she says in a tiny, shaky voice. 'It's so hard to do it all *alone*.'

Later, when Jane tiptoes into the bedroom to check on Misti and me, I close my eyes and steady my breathing and pretend I'm asleep. It's only after Jane's left, after I hear the outside door click shut and the sound of her car on the gravel drive, when I know she's gone back to her husband and her smart flat on the posh side of town, that I let the tears come.

18

Dear Gran,

Mum said she would ring you last week to tell you all about the move, but I'm wondering if maybe she forgot, because we haven't heard from you and Mum is kind of forgetful just now. Anyway, in case she did forget, our new address is 33 Hartington Drive and it's a bit of a dump but we've got it sorted pretty much.

Maybe you could come down and stay with us sometime? That would be great.

I miss you, Gran. I reckon Misti does too.

Well, I suppose I'm really writing to tell you my news. Guess what? I got the lead role in the school play! It's *Oliver!*, so I get to wear raggedy trousers and hide all my hair in a big tweed cap. I also get to sing a solo, which is very scary but Miss McDougall says we're not allowed to be scared, we have a show to put on, and we have to get on with it. So I suppose I will.

I had to audition for the play, and me and another girl called Aisha got the top part. We have to share it — she plays it one night, I play it the next. I was so proud on Friday when I heard, but my best friend, Jo (remember her?), didn't get a part so I couldn't really get excited about it or anything. It wouldn't have been fair on her, would it?

So I ran home to tell Mum and Misti, but guess what, I was unlucky again, because Mum was in bed with flu. I told Misti and we danced around and had a laugh, but when I told Mum she didn't really understand, or maybe she didn't hear, I don't know.

So that's another reason why I'm writing, because Mum's not well, and Jane says she's emotionally exhausted and very stressed and time is the best healer. I think she's missing Max, so maybe we'll end up back there anyway in the end. I'm not really sure.

It's not like this is a great flat or anything, but at least there's no fighting. I don't know if you knew about all that. Maybe I shouldn't say anything. It's not like it was all the time, anyway.

Anyway, maybe, if you're not really busy or anything, you could come up for a few days and see us. It would be good for Misti to have someone around while Mum isn't well. I asked Jane if I should stay off school to mind her, but Jane said no, best not. Mum'll be better soon, she said. Then she'll get a job and get back on top of things and maybe stop crying all the time.

If you did come, you could have my room. I mean, you'd have to share the bed with Misti, but she's pretty small, isn't she? Wriggly, though! I can sleep on the floor, or in Mum's bed if she falls asleep in the chair again. She keeps doing that lately.

We could go to the cinema and go swimming and make blackcurrant cheesecake like we do in Wales when we come down to visit. It'd be great.

I bet you won't recognize me, I'm loads taller than last summer, and Misti can talk now — she jabbers on all day long, and she smiles all the time. Well, maybe not just lately, but she'll be fine once Mum's better.

I hope you can make it. I can't wait to see you. Please come, if you can.

Love from Indie

xxxxxxxxxxxxxx

I fold up the letter and hide it under my pillow. All I need to do now is find an envelope and a stamp, and then decide whether to send it or not.

Maybe Mum'll be better soon, and I won't need to.

19

Jane calls over at lunchtime with croissants and butter and apricot jam. She feeds Mum coffee and drags her up from the chair where she slept, runs her a bath and tells her to get washed and dressed. Then she takes me and Misti out to the park.

Misti plays on the swings and Jane pushes her till she screams with joy. After a while, she gangs up with a bunch of toddlers going headfirst down the slide, crawling through the tunnels, leaping across sandpits. Jane and I sit on the grass.

'You OK?' she asks.

'Yeah, sure.'

I'm not, I know, but where do you start? It's not like Jane can change anything. She can't make Mum fall out of love with Max.

'Anna'll be fine,' Jane says. 'She's been through a lot, and maybe it's only just hit her. She needs some time to get herself sorted, get strong again. Hang on in there.'

'Right.'

Jane explains that Mum never got around to signing on for social security money, or help with the rent, and that's why the money's run out. Jane's going to sort it on Monday, first thing – get the forms, get things moving. Meanwhile, she gives me two powercards and two phonecards and five quid in silver in case we run out of milk or bread again.

'Ring me any time,' she says. 'I mean it, Indie, any time. If I'm not there, leave a message on the answerphone and I'll be round as soon as I can. And look, if you can't talk to me, at least talk to *someone*. Anyone. You can't cope with all this on your own. It's too much.'

I take the fiver and the cards and I take the bit of paper with Jane's scrawled number, but I don't take the advice. Who am I going to talk to about the mess my life has turned into? Who is going to care?

Later, back home, Jane and Mum are doing heart-to-hearts while Misti makes potato prints all over a vast roll of computer paper.

I'm sick of being bored. Why can't we have a TV, a computer, a phone?

I'm fed up being babysitter, fed up being sensible and sympathetic and endlessly under-standing. I'm mad at Mum for getting us mixed up with Max, making a mess of it all. I'm mad with her for being so weak, for wanting him back even though she knows he's a loser.

'No homework, Indie?' Jane asks, watching me sulk around the flat.

We're meant to be working on our Victorian projects, but I haven't started mine because I forgot to go to the library. At least, I didn't forget, exactly, I just didn't get to fit it in, between looking after Misti and worrying about Mum and Max and Jo.

How else am I meant to find out about the Victorians? The flicker of an idea starts to form in my mind.

I lean against the gate of number 33 and start to draw the tall, spooky house. It's complicated. I sketch in Ian Turner's tiny attic window, poking up out of the grey slate roof. I draw the two windows beneath, both with balconies. If we lived there, we'd have a table and chairs and plants and little jam-jar lanterns like the ones we once made at school with tea lights and wire and glass paint. I think it's students living on that floor, though. One balcony has a rusty bike, a clothes airer and a stepladder, all draped with washing. The other is bare, but the French window is ajar and waves of thumping, howling music float down on the breeze.

On the ground floor, there's Mrs Green's lace-curtained window with an ugly vase of yellow and orange flowers in the centre. The curtain twitches slightly as I look, but I don't care. I sketch in the front door with its peeling paint and the six doorbells with names and numbers scrawled beside them. I sketch the window on the far side, all dusty and cobwebby, with a broken pane of glass boarded up with chipboard. I bet Mrs Green wonders how it all happened, her once-posh house reduced to a student dive.

The front door opens a crack. 'What do you think you're doing?' Mrs Green shouts over crossly. 'Hanging about on street corners, staring in at me for hours on end. I could call the police!'

She shuffles over in her tartan slippers, her face furious. As she gets closer, I can see how old she is, much older than my gran. It looks like it hurts her to walk. Maybe that's why she's so crabby?

'I'm just drawing,' I say, showing her the picture. It's not very good, I know, but it's hardly a criminal offence.

'Why?' she barks.

'It's homework. We're doing a project on the Victorians, but I haven't had a chance to go to the library yet. So I'm drawing the house because Mum says it's Victorian.'

Mrs Green makes a harrumphing noise, like I've just admitted to something very stupid. She folds her arms and sniffs and looks at the drawing. She smells of powder and hairspray and too much perfume, and I notice that her lipstick, a kind of sickly Barbie pink, has spread out over her lips and sunk into the tiny cracks and wrinkles round her mouth.

After a minute or two, I carry on sketching. I put in the steps, the overgrown bushes, the glimpses of basement window behind them. I do the wheelie bins, the litter, the gravel drive.

'It was built in 1852,' Mrs Green announces suddenly. 'My great-great-grandfather, William Henry Poole, lived in it then. He owned the old factory in Rathbone Street, you know.'

'Oh,' is all I can think of to say.

'You've missed out the chimneys,' she says tartly, and shuffles back to the steps. 'William Henry Poole,' she says again, and slams the door.

I take my drawing inside, sharpen my pencil crayons and colour it in carefully, remembering to put in the fancy pattern in the brickwork with red and cream-coloured bricks, and the ivy creeping up the right-hand side of the house.

On a fresh sheet, I make a heading, *33 Hartington Drive*, and write down about Mrs Green's great-great-grandfather and the factory in Rathbone

Street and the date 1852. It might not be what Miss McDougall asked for, but it's better than nothing, isn't it?

Miss McDougall gives me a star for my project homework, and tells everybody that researching original material is an excellent way to find out about the Victorians.

'Swot,' Jo says.

And even though I get 7/20 for my maths test without even trying, she won't forgive me.

At lunchtime, we sit at the side of the playground in silence, Jo and Aisha and me. Jo paints her own nails 'Sizzling Sunset', then puts the bottle away pointedly.

'How was swimming club on Saturday?' I ask, desperate for something to say that won't spark off World War III. 'Did you . . . do any good strokes?'

Jo looks at me like I'm insane. She may not be too far off the mark.

'Erm, it was OK,' Aisha says brightly. 'I did mainly front crawl. But I'm in a different group from Jo –'

'You two are so – *boring*!' Jo bursts out. 'You just run around sucking up to Miss McDougall, showing off about the play, telling everyone how great you are. Well, you are *way* off the mark. You can't sing, you can't act, and Shane Taggart definitely doesn't fancy you. So *there*!'

She storms off, flicking back her hair and wiggling her bum in case Shane's watching.

Aisha and I look at each other, speechless. I'm horrified.

Aisha's mouth opens, then closes again. It twitches at the corners. If I smiled, or raised my eyebrows, or let my eyes sparkle at Aisha, she'd be laughing, I know. She'd nudge me and we'd double up together, giggling and spluttering at the cheek of it, the unfairness of it. But . . .

I want Jo back, my best, best mate.

I want her back the way she used to be, confident, careless, fun. I want her back the way she was before Aisha, before Shane, before the move.

Jo tries a hundred different tactics to pay me back.

She's mad at me because of Shane and because of Miss McDougall and the part of Oliver. She's punishing me.

I wish I could tell her how bad things are at home, how lost I'm feeling, how scared. I wish she could see how I feel. I wish she could see *me*.

She isn't even looking.

On Tuesday, she sits by Carrie Naughton all day. At breaktime I hear her swearing – Jo Ashton, the girl who still says 'Gosh' and 'Goodness' and 'Rats' when things go wrong. It doesn't sound right. It doesn't sound like Jo.

On Wednesday, she sits by Aisha. Aisha shrugs her shoulders and shakes her head at me when Jo's not looking, by way of apology. But it's not her fault. It's not her fault my best mate has dumped me.

On Thursday, she asks Shane Taggart out. He doesn't really fancy her, Buzz tells Aisha. But it's hard to say no to Jo Ashton, a fact I learned way back in Reception. It takes a stronger man than Shane.

Carrie Naughton tells everyone that Jo and Shane went behind the school kitchens and snogged till the bell went for afternoon class.

'Do you mind?' Aisha asks me.

'No! I don't even like him, I keep trying to tell you. And Jo really does, so maybe this will make her feel better. I hope so.'

I do hope so, but even though I can't tell Aisha, there's still a tiny part of me that feels betrayed. By Jo, because she's doing this to hurt me, to show me, to prove a point. And by Shane, because I know he likes me and I know he doesn't like Jo, not the same way.

So what's he doing snogging her behind the kitchens?

'Boys,' Aisha says gloomily. 'They're all the same.'

I'm feeling pretty punished now. I wish Jo would stop. She doesn't.

On Friday, she pulls the rabbit out of the hat.

She tells everyone who will listen that Mum's left Max, that we're living in a dank, dark cellar with fungus on the walls. She says she feels sorry for me, because it's tough when your mum can't stick with one bloke. It's tough when you don't even know who your father is.

My heart hits the concrete playground, splat. I can't see it, because hearts aren't like that, but I can feel it all right.

Did she mean me to hear?

Her eyes catch mine and I know that she did.

Aisha sees me standing still, frozen in time. The colour drains from my face, my heart turns to ice, my body feels stiff and cold and heavy, like a drowned person.

She puts an arm round me and steers me away, out of the playground, down across the grass to the far corner of the playing fields.

'If you want to cry, it's OK,' Aisha says. 'I won't tell anyone.'

But I can't cry. If I let the tears fall now, they'll never stop. Tears of anger, tears of self-pity. Tears for Jo, for Mum, for Max.

I can't.

'I'm OK,' I tell her. 'I'm just – shocked. She was my *friend*.'

Was.

'She didn't mean it,' Aisha says helplessly.

'She *did*.'

We sit for ages in the long grass, backs against the boundary fence.

I remember a day back in Year Three, when Miss Appleton was away and we had a supply teacher: a stern, speccy lady with a crew cut and a flowery blouse. It was the summer Danny left us and went to live back in Wales. I was sad that summer, but I knew Danny loved me even if he didn't love Mum. I knew we'd be OK.

The supply teacher asked us to make Father's Day cards, though, and I said I didn't want to.

'He's still your dad,' Jo had said. 'Even if he's gone, he's still your dad. Nothing can change that.'

'He's not,' I said in a small voice. 'Not really.'

'He is so,' Jo said.

'No,' I said. 'He really isn't.'

So I told Jo about Danny, how he met Mum when I was two years old, how we lived together, the three of us, in a tiny cottage on the Welsh coast, all rainbow stripes and tie-dyed bedsheets and music festivals in the summer. When we moved up to the north of England, it was a caravan at first, then a council flat. Danny cut his hair and got a job as a carpenter, but he wasn't happy, not really. He moved back to Wales and left us alone.

'He's not my dad,' I said to Jo again.

'Sorry. I didn't know,' she said. She was silent for a long time, colouring in.

'Who is, then?' she asked eventually. 'Who is your dad?'

I'd wanted to tell her something sad, something tragic, something glamorous, heroic, brave. I couldn't think of anything.

'I don't know,' I'd said.

Now, I lean back against the fence and hug my knees. When you look closely, the long grass is full of litter.

'Everything's gone wrong,' I say heavily.

'I know,' says Aisha, with feeling.

I know now that my dad was called Blue, that he and Mum met up at Glastonbury Festival and fell in love. Trouble is, it was a two-day kind of love, a nice-while-it-lasted romance. They didn't swap addresses. It wouldn't have mattered, except for me, the baby who appeared nine months later, growing up, asking awkward questions.

I know his name was Blue, but that's all.

'I *don't* know who my dad is,' I say.

Aisha shrugs. 'I don't know *where* mine is,' she says.

I frown. 'Isn't he at home? Or at work, you know?'

'No. He left us, six months ago. Mum thinks he's gone back to India. That's why we came here, so Mum could be near her parents. It's weird, though. She won't talk about it. It's like she's ashamed or something. And if anyone asks about Dad, everyone says he's away on business, even though he's not. Why can't people just tell the truth?'

'I dunno,' I say. 'Sorry, Aisha, about your dad. I never realized.'

'What difference does it make?'

I shrug. 'None, I s'pose.'

'See? It's you that matters in the end,' she says. 'Doesn't matter who your dad was. Doesn't matter about your mum and her ex. Doesn't matter if your flat's got fungus in the bathroom.'

'It *hasn't*,' I protest.

'Well then,' says Aisha. 'There you go. Could be worse.'

The bell goes for lessons and we leg it back up the playing field, but everyone's inside and sitting down by the time we hurtle into the classroom, red-faced and out of breath.

'Sorry, Miss McDougall,' says Aisha.

'Humphhh,' says Miss McDougall. 'Don't let it happen again.'

Jo's sitting by Aisha's desk, beaming out a sparkly smile. 'I got your stuff out,' she whispers to Aisha.

'Thanks.'

I slump down into my chair and wonder when the hurt will go away, but then Aisha dumps her bag on Jo's old desk and flops down next to me, grinning. Miss McDougall shoots a withering glance at Jo, Aisha and me in turn.

'I don't know what's going on,' she booms. 'But this musical chairs business stops – today. Understood?'

'Yes, Miss McDougall,' Aisha and I chorus.

'Sorry, Miss,' Aisha adds for good measure.

Jo's silent, glowering, but I'm past feeling sorry for her now.

She's not worth it.

And I have Aisha sitting next to me, who doesn't fuss and flounce and play silly payback games. It feels OK.

21

Mum is ill for a week, maybe two. It may not be flu, but she's ill all the same, and it's scary. She sleeps a lot and she cries a lot, and often, when I get home from school, she looks like she's just got out of bed.

Some days Misti is bathed and clean, and dressed in her spotty tights and her turquoise pinafore and her flowery top. She plays with her crayons and her collage stuff and her play dough, and she seems OK. Other days, I get home from school and she's grubby and tear-stained, her face smeared with jam or Marmite.

Sometimes she's still in her pyjamas, and sometimes she's wet or dirty because Mum forgot to change her nappy. Those nights, I make beans on toast or cheese on toast for tea, then dump Misti in the bath with all her dolls and treat her to a squoosh of my peachy bubble bath and let her borrow my dolphin facecloth.

Jane comes every other night, sometimes with chips, sometimes with pizza, once with a Chinese takeaway that nobody liked. She makes sure there's always cash in the emergency blue purse. She makes sure there's always at least one spare powercard. She makes sure Mum gets dressed and the two of them talk and talk, and Mum promises not to ring Max again.

I don't tell Jane about the nights that Mum sneaks out of the flat when she thinks I'm asleep. She's never gone for long, maybe ten, twenty minutes, just long enough to walk down to the phone box. I lie awake, watching the minutes tick by, until I hear the door click shut and I know she's home again, safe and sound.

Jane remembers to pay the rent before Mrs Green gets in a tizz, and then at last Mum's money comes through and she seems a bit better. We do a big shop in the supermarket, bulk-buying nappies and pasta and peanut butter and jam.

We're loading up the pushchair with carrier bags when we see Ian Turner, smart and smiley in his blue business suit, marching along behind the tills.

'Hello, Mr Turner,' I say, and he stops, grinning.

'Ian,' he corrects, pointing to a little red badge on his lapel.

Ian, Customer Services, it says.

'I didn't know you worked here,' I say.

'You do now! It's a dirty job, but someone's got to do it,' he jokes. He looks at Mum. You can tell he likes her, just from the way he looks.

'Well, at least that flu's gone,' he says. 'You're looking great.'

Mum goes pink. She does look OK, though. Her hair is clean and shiny, drifting loose across the shoulders of her blue velvet top. Her old jeans, patched and faded, are tucked into the tops of her blue suede boots.

'Can I give you a lift home with the shopping at all?' Ian asks. 'I can drop it off later, no hassles. Then this little lady won't have to balance a bag of nappies on her knee . . .'

He produces a wrapped fudge from his pocket and pretends to magic it from Misti's ear, making her giggle.

'Bet you're too old for tricks like that,' he says to me. He fiddles about by my ear for a moment. 'Yup, thought so. Nothing there.'

Why do people always think eleven is too old for magic?

'We'll be fine, Mr Turner – *Ian*,' Mum is saying. 'You've done so much for us already, I really can't thank you enough. But we'll walk home today – we'll enjoy it, won't we, girls?'

I nod, hooking Misti by the hand. She beams

at him, her mouth already brown and sticky with fudge.

'OK, then, see you around, Anna,' he says.

'Bye, Ian.'

As we walk away I find a wrapped fudge in my pocket. I turn to shout thank you, but Ian has disappeared.

When we get home, Mum makes up a bag of groceries to replace the stuff Ian gave us. She adds a bottle of cheap wine instead of the chocolate and gets me to leave it on the front doorstep with a big label attached.

As I'm sneaking away, the door snaps open and I'm collared by Mrs Green. 'I've been looking for you,' she says crossly.

'Oh?' I swallow hard. She smells of mint humbugs today.

'Come inside.'

I feel like Hansel and Gretel in Misti's book of fairy tales, wandering into the witch's house. We creep across the tatty hallway and Mrs Green opens her door wide. Inside, her flat's stuffed with lumpy, chintz-covered chairs and side tables piled up with china ornaments. The walls, papered in something swirling and mustard coloured, are crammed with old paintings in heavy frames, em-broidered samplers and cute kitten-in-the-basket calendars for years long gone.

'Sit down,' Mrs Green commands, and I balance nervously on the edge of a hard, tweedy armchair with shiny polished arms. Is she going to tell me off? Offer me Earl Grey tea and cucumber sandwiches? Ask me why Mum was round the back of the house last Sunday morning, digging weeds out of flower beds, dressed in her nightie?

She scrabbles around in a drawer for a moment.

'Ah, here they are.'

It's photos. Mrs Green is showing me thick, creased, faded brown photos from a million years BC. One shows a frowny man in a moustache and top hat, sitting by a big potted plant. Another shows an older Mr Moustache, this time with a curly-fringed wife in a button-up dress with a skirt that sticks out at the back. Three frowny children, two boys dressed in white-collared suits and a girl in a ruffle-necked frock, stand stiff and still beside them.

'Mr William Henry Poole,' the old lady explains. 'My great-great-grandfather.'

So *that's* where she gets the frowny face.

Then she shows me a sheet of lined paper, filled with spidery handwriting. It's a family tree.

'Right,' I say, baffled. 'Very nice.'

Mrs Green points out William Henry Poole, hovering near the top of the tree with Matilda Johanna Poole (née Wilmott). Then she traces a path downwards to Audrey Louisa Green (née Poole).

'That's me,' she says.

'Oh.'

Mrs Green puts the photographs and the family tree into a padded envelope and hands it to me.

'For your school project,' she says. 'All the dates are there, so you can see exactly who lived here in Victorian times. Will it be useful, do you think?'

'Yes, thank you, Mrs Green,' I say, amazed.

'Take care of it, now,' she barks.

'I will.'

Mrs Green offers me a mint humbug on the way out. She's not *so* bad, I suppose.

One afternoon, I get home from a late rehearsal and find Mum and Ian Turner chatting and drinking mugs of coffee in the kitchen.

'How'd it go?' Mum asks, pouring me a glass of milk and shaking the biscuit tin. 'Indie's got the lead part in the school play, you know,' she says to Ian. 'She's going to be Oliver.'

'A star in the making,' Ian Turner says. 'When's the big night?'

I tell him. Not so far away as it seemed before. Not so far away at all.

'Get me a ticket, OK?' Ian says. 'I'd love to see it. I want a good seat, mind, in the middle, near the front, next to this very beautiful young lady . . .' He ruffles Misti's hair and breaks off a sneaky piece of biscuit for her.

'OK.'

I think Mum's feeling better.

*

Miss McDougall gives me a star for bringing in the photos of William Henry Poole, and helps me photocopy them in the school office. She tells me to copy out the family tree, underlining the Victorians in red gel pen. Mum suggests drawing a big, leafy tree-shape round it, plus a gnarled old trunk and wiggly roots.

I look at the photocopied image of William Henry Poole and Matilda Johanna Poole and their three frowny-faced kids (Albert, Edward and Julia). What did it feel like to be eleven years old 150 years ago? Miss McDougall says that life Wasn't Easy back then. I wish someone would tell her that's it's not exactly a picnic now.

'Think hungry,' Miss McDougall says when Aisha and I are acting out the workhouse scenes. 'Think lonely, think lost,' she says when we're trying to put some feeling into Oliver's solo song. 'Think scared,' she says when we're acting out the bit where Oliver gets stolen away by Bill Sykes, or the bit where Bill kills Nancy and Oliver can't do a thing to stop it happening.

I can do all that. I can do hungry, lonely, lost, scared, and more.

'Good girl, Indie,' Miss McDougall says. 'Good *girl.*'

We have rehearsals after school every Monday and Friday. It's not so hard to learn all those words, not when you're all in it together, scene after scene. It gets so it's like a story running in your head, a Disney film you know by heart, a nursery rhyme you can say forwards, backwards, sideways.

We have singing practice with the whole class every afternoon, just for half an hour, till we know all the songs. Miss McDougall says we need more practice, but you can tell she's pleased. Sometimes, Aisha and me have extra practice at lunchtimes, polishing up the solo song or going over some tricky scene.

Miss McDougall sets a competition to design a poster for the show, and Iqbal wins with a drawing of a sad-eyed boy holding out a bowl. Miss Kearns and Mr Leonie are painting backdrops for us, and Kai's mum comes in and measures everyone for costumes. We get a letter home, asking if anyone's parents can help with the sewing, and Mum says she'll have a go.

Miss McDougall sends her acres of sugar-pink lining fabric and a sample dress, and she stitches ten girly frocks for the flower-seller scene in just one week.

Mum's up every morning now, before I go to school, making porridge with a swirl of honey, pouring orange juice, tidying the flat. She sleeps, she eats, she even laughs. She keeps Misti clean and tidy, plays with her, goes to the park, takes her to toddler group. She gets the shopping every day, she washes and irons, she makes soup and stew and macaroni cheese and apple crumble with custard. She's stopped crying the whole time, and she never talks about Max any more.

She never sneaks out late at night, when she thinks I'm asleep, to ring him.

Sometimes she fetches shopping for Mrs Green, or sits up late drinking coffee and laughing with Ian Turner.

Jane's stopped worrying. I've stopped worrying. We're free.

Mum notices that I haven't been to Jo's house for a very long time. 'It's OK, you know, if you want to,' she says. 'I'm OK now, really. I know how wonderful you've been, keeping things together here, looking after Misti. I'm sorry I put you through that, Indie. But it's fine now. Go and enjoy yourself a bit. Go to Jo's.'

I shrug.

'Or ask her here again, if that's easier? We could have pizza, make popcorn . . .'

'I don't see Jo much any more,' I say.

OK, I see her every day, but I can't look at her. If she walks towards me, my eyes slide away and I turn my back. There are only so many times you can lie down flat and let someone walk all over you.

Mum looks stricken. 'Oh, Indie, love, I had no idea . . .'

She puts her arms round me for a moment and we cling on, squeezing hard. Misti comes up, looking anxious, and burrows into the middle of us. We're a blonde-haired, blue-eyed, messed-about sandwich.

When we break away, Mum makes hot chocolate and floats marshmallows on the top. Misti's face is streaked with chocolate and goo.

'Mum . . .'

'Yup?'

'Could I ask someone else? Could I ask someone else to tea?'

Aisha walks home with me after rehearsals on Friday, and she doesn't moan about how far it is or tell me I'll have to go to Rathbone High. She likes 33 Hartington Drive.

'It's huge,' she says in awe. 'Really spooky, just like your drawing.'

When the curtain twitches and Mrs Green waves, I wave back, and Aisha joins in. 'Is she the landlady?' Aisha wants to know. 'I thought you said she was mean and scary?'

'Oh, she'd like to be,' I say. 'But she's not. We keep the flower beds at the back weeded and buy her mint humbugs, and she's a pussycat.'

'Oh.'

Aisha likes the flat too.

'Definitely no fungus,' she says, eyeing the walls. 'It's huge! Oh wow, your room is so *cool*!'

Last week, while I was at school, Mum painted bluebirds all round the doorway, swooping and diving and dipping down towards the skirting boards. Once she'd checked I liked it, she added a scattering of bluebells growing up from the floorboards.

Aisha's right, it's cool.

We eat pizza and shop-bought cream cakes, and sip hot chocolate with melted marshmallows because Aisha's never tried it before. Then we make popcorn and Ian Turner comes round just in time to share. Aisha and I steal a dish of hot, buttery corn and flop down in my room playing CDs. Misti charges in and we dress her up as a fairy, all pink net and fluffy wings. I make her a wand from card, silver glitter and a green garden stick, and Aisha makes a crown out of sweet wrappers, dried pasta and the back of the cornflakes box. Misti tiptoes away to cast spells on Mum and Ian.

'She's so cute,' Aisha says. 'Your sister. I wish I had a sister.'

'You can have Misti . . .'

'Nah. Really. *So* cute. And your mum is really

nice, really young and pretty. She likes blue, doesn't she? The colour blue?'

'Mmmm. A fortune-teller told Mum that blue was her lucky colour, when she was sixteen. She always wears blue. Blue boots, blue skirts, blue jeans, blue tops, blue jackets. That's why she called me Indigo, why Misti is Misti. I suppose we should be grateful she didn't name us Ultraviolet and Navy, or Turquoise and Sky.'

We giggle. I don't mention that I've often wondered if Mum fell for Blue because of his name. I couldn't exactly have a dad called Red, could I? And Danny, he had blue-dyed dreadlocks. Even Max has a blue builder's van and blue eyes. Scary-blue, piercing, ice-blue.

'It's so romantic,' Aisha sighs. 'Does it work?'

'Does what work?'

'Does it bring her luck?'

I pull a face.

'What do *you* think?'

23

Mum has a job.

She's working at the supermarket, part-time, so she starts at ten and finishes at three, just in time to meet me from school on the days when I'm not rehearsing. Misti gets to stay in the supermarket crèche while Mum works, and she loves it. Everyone is happy.

Mum looks very young and sweet in her little white cap, her hair scraped up into a bun or a spiral of plaits. She wears a candy-striped nylon tabard over her blue top and skirt, a red enamel name badge like Ian's. It says, *Anna, Store Assistant*.

The first week, Mum stacks shelves and moves boxes around in the warehouse. She meets me at school every afternoon, her eyes bright, her cap and her tabard folded neatly in her blue suede shoulder bag. Misti curls up in the pushchair, pink-faced and happy.

Every time, Mum produces a different treat for

the long walk home. An iced bun, a punnet of strawberries, French bread still warm from the bakery ovens.

The second week, Mum gets to work in the supermarket cafe, clearing the tables and wiping up spills and emptying the dishwasher. She likes that too. She brings home egg mayonnaise baguettes that didn't sell in time, and chocolate muffins, Danish pastries, a whole cheese-and-onion quiche.

'You wouldn't believe the stuff they give away at the end of each shift,' she tells me. 'Just to make sure the food on sale is ultra-fresh. We can eat like kings.'

The third week, she's put on the checkouts. It's easy, she says. The computerized till does all the hard work, and she just has to scan the bar codes and say friendly things to the customers.

And when her pay cheque comes, at the end of the month, we're going to be *rich*.

They ask Mum to work the morning shift on Saturday, pay day, to cover for a girl who's off sick. Mum agrees.

'Don't let them take advantage,' Ian tells her. 'Tell them you need Saturdays for your kids.'

'I know, I know,' Mum says. 'Next time, I will. Promise.'

Ian laughs. 'I know,' he grins. 'Heard it all

before. I'm working the early shift on Saturday too.'

Misti and I go to Jane's on Saturday, and Jane shows us how to make gingerbread. Misti makes gingerbread blobs and gingerbread lumps, and I use a small, sharp knife to cut out a wobbly gingerbread man specially for Mum. We bake them in Jane's posh oven, watching through the smoked-glass door till they're just the right shade of golden brown.

We watch cartoons on Jane's TV while the cookies cool, then tear open the pack of coloured icing tubes she's bought to decorate them. I use white icing to pipe collar, cuffs and buttons on my beautiful, wobbly gingerbread man. I use green for his eyes, red for his lips, blue for his belt and shoes. Misti ices her cookies with a frenzy of splotches and swirls, and has to be swabbed down with a warm flannel.

'OK, girls,' Jane announces after another dose of cartoons. 'Time to go shopping. Time to meet Anna!'

The plan is to go get Jane's shopping and see Mum in action at the checkout, then have lunch at the supermarket cafe.

We pack the cookies into a tin, strap Misti into the pushchair and set off.

Jane gets a different kind of shopping from

us. She buys wine and profiteroles and ciabatta bread and lots of ready-cooked meals from the freezer cabinet. At 2.25 exactly, we line up at Mum's checkout.

'Terrible weather for June,' Mum says as she packs groceries for the woman ahead of us. 'Rain again. Isn't it dreadful? Ooh, sweet potatoes – have you tried them before? How do you cook them?'

She winks at us, handing Jane a plastic sign that says *This Till is Now Closed*.

She swishes everything past the scanner neatly, so that the bar codes bleep and the prices flash up. Then she swipes Jane's credit card through the till, waits for the signature and helps us pack up the shopping.

'Meet you in the cafe, Anna,' Jane says, steering us away. 'I'll just have a coffee, then I have to dash – Bob and I are shopping for a sofa this afternoon.'

'Sure – won't be five minutes,' Mum says. 'I'll just cash up. I've got my shopping already, I just need to pick it up from the office.'

We order sausage, chips and beans, with strawberry tarts for pudding, and ice-cold milk in big paper cups. Jane pays for everything on her card while I grab cutlery, salt and pepper, tomato sauce.

'Done,' sighs Mum, slipping into the seat opposite Jane. She dumps three bags of groceries and a vast bag of nappies on to the floor. Not the cheap brand we usually get, I notice. The biggest and best.

Another bag is topped with a box of warm jam doughnuts. A third holds lemonade, garlic bread, bubble bath, a teen mag for me. Pay-day shopping.

'Boy, did that shift go on forever,' Mum says. 'Thank you, Jane, for minding the girls. For everything. You're the best friend ever.'

'Hey, I thought that was *me*,' Ian Turner says, stopping beside our table, a laden tray balancing dangerously in the air. 'Shove up, Indie.'

Jane raises her eyebrows and Mum goes slightly pink. 'You know Ian, don't you, Jane? I asked him to join us,' she says.

'Hi there,' Jane says. 'Heard lots about you.'

Ian pulls a terrified face and sits down between me and Misti. Straight away, he tries to nick her sausage. She squeals with delight, and lets Ian feed her forkfuls of banger. In return, she feeds him soggy, sauce-drenched chips.

'Well, anyway, Anna, no hassles about this morning,' Jane says. 'Any time.' She drains her coffee.

'Gotta go now,' she grins, grabbing her bag and car keys. 'I have a date with a big, squashy sofa and a big, handsome man.'

'Sounds interesting,' Ian says.

'Expensive,' Jane corrects him. 'We're buying a new suite. Call me, Anna.'

'I will,' Mum promises, and we wave till Jane's out of sight.

Ian and Mum tuck into fish 'n' chips, then big slabs of chocolate gateau.

'I'll never eat all this, Ian,' Mum protests, but she does all the same. Ian orders two more cappuccinos.

'We're celebrating,' he says. 'Anna's first pay packet at the supermarket. A brilliant start to the job, so I've been told.'

'We've got doughnuts for tea,' I say. 'And lemonade.'

'Have we?'

Ian looks so smiley, it seems mean not to ask him down to share it.

'After all, you did tell me about the job,' Mum says.

'But *you* got it,' he points out. 'You've stuck with it.' He raises his mug in the air.

'To Anna,' he toasts. 'The cutest checkout girl ever to live at 33 Hartington Drive.'

'The *only* checkout girl ever to live ...' Mum starts to correct him, but suddenly her voice trails away and her face is white, frozen, still.

'Anna?' Ian nudges her. 'What's up? You OK?'

But still she stares into the distance, her eyes

wide, her coffee mug stranded halfway to her mouth.

'Mum?'

She drops the mug suddenly, spilling a last trickle of cappuccino over the tabletop. Grabbing a handful of napkins, she mops at the spill, fingers trembling.

'Sorry – oh, sorry, I just thought – but no, it can't have been. It can't. It's OK, really. I'm sorry.'

I'm on my feet, looking into the distance too, but there's nobody there. I know who I'm looking for, though. Max. He wouldn't come here. Would he?

Ian pushes the loaded trolley while Mum steers the buggy.

'Hang on,' Ian tells us, just outside the office near the door. 'Left my jacket.'

He reappears a minute later with the biggest bunch of flowers I've ever seen. Red roses, pink carnations, clouds of starry white flowers on spider-thin stems.

'For my three favourite girls,' he tells us, bowing low, but he hands the bouquet to Mum alone.

'Ian, you shouldn't have . . .'

'They were reduced,' he says. 'Past their sell-by date.'

'And I'm the queen of China,' Mum says.

'At your service, Your Majesty,' Ian says. 'Your carriage awaits.'

Mum doesn't argue about the lift this time. She lets Ian load the bags of shopping into the boot of his red Fiat. He unlocks the doors and we pile inside, stretching out on the plush seats. I pull Misti on to my lap and wrap the seat belt round the two of us.

The car floods with music as we ride home through the Saturday streets. Ian says he'll order in a pizza if we promise to bring up our box of doughnuts and the bottle of lemonade. He stops by the video shop and lets us choose a video each. Mum picks *Chocolat* and I pick *Oliver!* and Misti takes ages to decide between *Cinderella* and *The Lion King*, but Ian doesn't get impatient.

'We'll have *The Lion King* next week,' he promises.

Mum catches his eye and whispers, 'Thank you,' as he checks out the videos. It feels like a private moment. It feels like I shouldn't be watching.

Only once, as we drive home laughing through the drizzly afternoon, do I think I see a blue van following behind, at a distance. But I know I'm just imagining things. I know I am.

After we unload the shopping, Mum and Ian decide they need more coffee, so Ian comes in and puts the kettle on. There's no vase for the flowers, so we prop them up in a saucepan in the centre of the table. Ian pulls out two pink carnations and sticks one behind Misti's ear, one behind mine.

'So. Anything you don't like on your pizza?' Ian asks. 'Pineapple? Salami? Extra onion?'

'No, we like everything,' Mum says happily. 'Don't we?'

'Jam,' says Misti, and wonders why we all start laughing.

'Chocolate spread,' I say. 'Vanilla ice cream.'

'Toothpaste,' Mum suggests. 'Pink carnations.'

'You'll be sorry you said that,' Ian grins, but doesn't look sorry, not a bit.

Ian says he's off to tidy up the flat a bit, and tells us to come up any time, half four, five-ish, whenever we want. We can watch Misti's video first and then order in the pizza.

He sticks his head back round the door. 'Don't forget the doughnuts!'

'If they *last* till then,' I shout.

The door slams shut. Mum starts putting away the shopping, stacking the tins neatly in the cupboard, the pasta high on the shelf. I remember the gingerbread cookies in their tin under the buggy. I fish them out, prise the lid off the tin.

'Guess what we made at Jane's?' I say, just as the doorbell rings. I ditch the cookie tin and go to the door.

'What's he forgotten *now*?' Mum calls out.

I open the door wide.

'Hi, Indie.'

It's Max.

He stands on the doorstep, smiling, effortlessly handsome in clean jeans and a tight black T-shirt.

'Hi,' I say listlessly. 'Hi, Max.'

Mum drifts over to the door, a hand over her mouth.

'Max.'

'Anna. Aren't you going to invite me in?'

Mum stands back and he strides in, looking around, wrinkling up his nose a bit at the damp smell that we've all got so good at ignoring.

'Nice place,' he says, not meaning it.

Max sits at the table and Mum makes yet more coffee.

I stand with my back against the kitchen cupboard, staying close to Mum, watching Max from a distance. Misti, wide-eyed and chewing at her pink bunny, clings to my leg.

'So. Haven't heard from you for a while, Anna. You stopped calling.'

'I thought it was for the best,' Mum says.

'Did you?' asks Max. 'I wonder. Best for who?'

'Best for everyone,' Mum says, but her voice wobbles slightly. She slumps down into the chair opposite Max, staring at him like a rabbit caught in the headlights of a truck.

'You're doing well for yourself, I hear,' Max says. 'Job, flat, boyfriend.'

'No boyfriend,' Mum says quickly. 'Who told you that? No boyfriend.'

'No? I'm glad they were wrong about that, at least,' Max says. 'That way I can kid myself you're still missing me, even just a bit. How about you, Indie? Misti? Have you missed me?'

He stretches out an arm and Mum nods at us to come forward. I have to drag Misti. Max pulls us into a quick bear hug, then releases us. It feels awkward, wrong.

'That's my girls,' Max says. 'The house is so

quiet without you. I messed up, Anna. How long are you going to go on punishing me?'

'I – I'm not,' Mum says, startled.

'It feels like it,' Max tells her. 'I got the message, and I've changed, really I have. I suppose I didn't know what I was losing till it was too late. Is it too late? Anna?'

'I don't know.'

There's a long silence. Max stares into his coffee mug, frowning.

'Can you give me another chance? Can we at least talk about this? For the kids' sake, even? Misti deserves to know who her dad is.'

Mum bites her lip. Misti crawls on to her lap, pulling at her hair, her face.

'I *love* you,' Max says. 'I love you all.'

Mum nods.

'Are you really going to throw all this away?' Max demands. 'Everything we had together? Without giving me a chance to make amends?'

A tear slides down Mum's pale cheek.

I'm trembling, sick with anger and fear and disgust.

'So,' says Max, suddenly brisk again. 'Who are the flowers from?'

'What? Oh, the flowers,' Mum says. 'They're – not mine. Not ours. Are they, Indie? They belong to the man upstairs. He gave us a lift home today, and he must have left the flowers by mistake . . .'

Mum's babbling, and Max sits back looking amused.

'So hadn't you better give them back?' Max asks. 'Tell him they're not wanted?'

'Yes, yes, I will . . .'

Mum lifts up the flowers, letting them drip all over the table.

'Indie, could you . . .?' she pushes them into my arms and I breathe in the sweet, heady smell. It's almost overwhelming.

Mum picks the carnation out from behind my ear and tries to hide it in her hand. Misti's has already disappeared.

'Tell Mr Turner thank you for the lift. Tell him we picked up his flowers by mistake . . .'

Behind Max's back, I try to mime eating pizza. 'What about the videos?' I say in a silent whisper. 'The pizza?'

'Not tonight,' Mum says, without making a sound. 'Not tonight.'

I run outside and up the big steps to the front door. I lean on Ian's doorbell till I hear his footsteps on the big, creaky stairs.

The door opens.

'Right,' says Ian. 'You're early. Got the dough-nuts?'

Then he sees the flowers.

'What's up, Indie? What's wrong?'

'Max is here,' I say. 'Max is Mum's boyfriend. Well, he *was*. He's Misti's dad.'

'So?'

'Well, he thinks you left the flowers at our house by mistake.'

I can't bring myself to say that he thinks that because it's what Mum told him.

'Does he now?'

'Mmmm. And Mum says we can't come up for pizza tonight, or videos. She's very, very sorry.'

'Right,' says Ian. 'Well, so am I. But another night, hey? No harm done.'

'No.'

He looks at me, disappointed but still smiling, a stripy apron tied round him, a duster in his hand.

He docsn't know, he hasn't got a clue.

'Everything OK, Indie?' he asks.

It's too long a story to even get started.

'Yeah, sure,' I say. 'Everything's fine.'

25

When I get back to the flat, Max is eating the big rainbow-coloured gingerbread man I made specially for Mum. He snaps its head off, chewing noisily. He dunks its blue icing feet in his second mug of coffee.

'Good stuff, Indie,' he says with his mouth full. 'You must have known I was coming.'

I wish.

We could have run away, or hidden in the bedrooms until the doorbell stopped ringing. We could have gone sofa-shopping with Jane, or flat-dusting with Ian. We could have gone out to the park and stayed till dark, creeping home only when the streets were quiet and empty and clear of big blue vans.

It's too late now. Mum's shining Saturday-morning face is closed and pale and anxious, her eyes tearful, her lips trembling.

'Come back,' Max says. 'Come back, Anna.'

'It's not that easy.'

'It *is* that easy. It really is,' Max says. 'Just fling a few things in a bag, hop in the van. We'll be home in ten minutes. We can come back next week, move the rest of your stuff – or ditch it – and everything's back to normal. The way it should be.'

Mum stares down at the tabletop. Misti, asleep in a sprawl in her arms, shifts silently, finds her thumb and starts to suck.

'What's stopping you?' Max says.

Mum shakes her head, buries her face in Misti's hair.

'Think of the kids,' Max appeals. 'What are you doing, Anna, making them live in this mould-ridden dump? Look at it. *Smell* it. It should have been condemned years ago.'

'I like it,' I say loyally, but Mum's urgent look silences me. It is a dump, I think sadly. It *does* smell, it *is* damp, and the furniture looks like we found it on a skip. But I like it.

Max doesn't take his eyes off Mum. 'Look, I made a mistake, I know it,' he says. 'I've changed, Anna, believe me. Come home. I want you home.'

I walk to the bedroom and switch on my CD player. I turn up the volume till I can't hear Max any more. I play the same CD three times over before I hear the door click shut. I peer out of the bedroom and see Mum alone at the table, her head in her hands.

'It's OK, Mum,' I say. 'He's gone.'

'I don't know what to do,' she says. 'I don't know how to make him *see*.'

'You don't have to,' I tell her gently. 'He's gone.'

'No, Indie,' Mum says. 'He's coming back.'

Max is taking Mum out for a meal, so they can talk properly. He wants to show her how much he's changed, how much he cares. He's going to talk and talk at her till he wears her down, wipes her out, makes her back into the person she used to be.

He's going to make us move back in.

'Don't go, Mum,' I say. 'Just *tell* him. We're OK here, aren't we?'

'Mmmm. But I have to go, Indie. Don't be scared – I'm not going back to him, I promise I'm not. I just need to explain, make him *see*. He's not a bad man, Indie, but it was a bad relation-ship. We're better off apart. I need to make him see that.'

Mum sounds so sussed, so strong. I almost believe that she's right, that she can do it. But then I remember Max, and the way he makes her curl up inside herself, sad and lost and weak.

I know it's not going to work.

146

Mum goes out to the phone box and calls Jane, to see if she'll come over and sit with us, but Jane isn't back.

'Maybe Misti and I could go up and do the video and pizza thing with Ian?' I suggest.

'I don't think so,' Mum says. 'His car's gone. He must have gone out. Anyway, Max wouldn't like it. No, I'll ring Jane back later.'

Max wouldn't like it?

And?

We search through Mum's cupboard to find something beautiful, blue and posh enough for a smart restaurant. Misti unearths a battered felt hat with a curling blue feather, and pulls it on. Her face disappears, and she squeals with glee. Mum lets her wear an old pair of floral blue Doc Martens to match.

We drag out a long, flippy skirt in dark, storm-blue velvet and a matching gypsy top. Its flared sleeves have tiny blue beads stitched along their edges. Mum irons it, then has a bath and gets changed. She looks like a princess.

'Boots or sandals?' she asks, and we all vote for the kitten-heeled sandals with the tiny blue-flower trim. Mum pins up her hair and ties a floaty scarf into it, the ends trailing down like a veil.

She takes a whole lot of trouble to look beautiful just to tell Max she's not coming back.

At half seven, Mum pulls on her jacket and runs round to the phone box. Again, she's back in minutes, frowning this time.

'Jane's still not in,' she says. 'I left a message, but . . . what shall I do?'

'We'll be OK,' I say bravely, not feeling it.

'No, no, I can't just leave you.'

The doorbell chimes and I feel all sad and panicky.

'Oh, Max,' Mum is saying. 'Jane's not back yet and I can't think who else to ask. I need *someone* to sit with the kids. What shall I do?'

'How about your friend with the flowers?' Max says, his lip curling a little.

'No, no. I hardly know him. And he's out tonight. And Mrs Green, she's just too old, she wouldn't be able to cope. And the students are never in at the weekend. There's nobody I can ask, Max. Maybe we should just . . .'

'No,' Max says. 'The table's booked for eight o'clock and we're *going*, Anna. It's important. It's our future.'

'I know, I know . . .'

'Indie's eleven,' Max says brightly. 'That's old enough to babysit. You can look after Misti, can't you? Just for an hour or so?'

I stare at Max. My cheeks feel pink, and my heart is thumping.

He throws an arm round my shoulder. 'You're a big girl now, aren't you, Indie? You'll do it, won't you, to give me and Anna a bit of space? We've got stuff to talk about, important stuff.'

I look at Mum. She looks away. I can't work out what she wants me to say.

'OK,' I say at last. 'Max is right, Mum, I'm easily old enough to babysit. We'll be fine, won't we, Misti? Honest.'

26

It takes another twenty minutes before we convince
Mum, but eventually she gives in, her hand wrapped
tight in Max's. She looks back over her shoulder,
waving, her face all white and sad and beautiful.

'Just you and me, Misti,' I say.

It's no big deal. I've been looking after Misti
for months, on and off. And Mum's been out
before and left us alone, even if it was only to walk
to the phone box on the corner. No big deal.

Misti peers up at me from under her blue
felt hat.

'Supper time,' I say.

We eat jam doughnuts and drink milk, cuddled
together in the big armchair in front of the three-
bar electric fire. I eat three doughnuts and Misti
manages four. She gets jam on her face, jam in her
hair, jam all over her clothes. She smears jam all
down my stripy top, dusts sugar across my nose
and cheeks.

Bathtime.

I've run half a bath full of water before I realize it's stone cold. Mum's used all the hot water. She must have switched the immersion heater off.

I drain the bath, and wet a flannel instead.

Misti doesn't like flannels, especially not cold ones. She screams and howls and wriggles free, and all I manage to do is dilute the jam smears and spread them about a bit more.

She's wet too. What with everything that's been happening this afternoon, maybe Mum forgot to change her.

I check in the bathroom for nappies, but there are none left. I look in the kitchen for the big new bag we bought earlier, but I can't find it. I hunt in the cupboards, root in the wardrobe, check under the bed. It's not here. It's not in the flat.

I think back to when we unloaded the car. We were laughing, joking, messing around. Maybe we forgot to unload the nappies. They're probably still in the boot of Ian's car, wherever that is. I stand on a chair and peer out through the high bedroom window. No red Fiat.

I check Mum's blue suede shoulder bag, in case there's a spare nappy hidden. There isn't.

I strip off Misti's soaking tights and chuck out the nappy. When I try to wash her with the cold flannel, she howls again, kicking and scratching, so I drag on her pyjama trousers anyway and let her go.

Within minutes, she's wet again and I have to peel off the pyjamas and scrub the place on the cheap blue carpet where she dripped. I dress her again in a clean pair of jammies and tell her it's time for bed.

'No,' Misti says. '*No*, Inky. No bed. Want Mummy.'

Her face, tired and jam-stained, threatens tears. 'No bed.'

I give in. We cuddle up on the big armchair with Misti's big book of fairy tales. She picks out *Rapunzel*. We're just at the bit where the wicked witch shuts Rapunzel in the tower when the lights flicker and go out.

We're sitting in darkness, watching the three-bar electric fire fade from red to orange to nothing at all.

Misti starts to roar.

'Hey, hey, hey!' I tell her. 'Don't panic, Misti, it's just that the leccy's gone. We need to find the spare powercard . . .'

It's in my school bag, along with Jane's purse of emergency cash and the phonecard she gave me weeks ago. I just have to get the torch and find it . . .

Misti is howling, clinging on to me like a

monkey. Every time I try to put her down, she pinches my arms, pulls my hair, kicks out at my ribs, my belly.

'Inky, *no!*' she screams. 'Want light! Want Mummy! Bad, *bad*, Inky!'

'Misti, let go . . . I need to find the torch . . .'

But she clings and screams and scratches and bites, trying to hang on in the dark.

I hoist her up on my hip and hold her as tightly as I can, stumbling around in the dark trying to find the torch. My eyes blink against a blanket of darkness, struggling to make sense of it. I finally get to the stripy cupboard and drag open the drawer.

Papers. Clothes pegs. Address book. No torch.

But this is where it *always* is.

'Oh, *Muu-um* . . .' My voice is a wail of despair.

Misti, hearing the panic, collapses on to my shoulder, limp and sobbing.

I bite my lip and check the other drawers. Tea towels, scrubbing brush, dishcloths. Paints, crayons, brushes, biros, sketchbook. No torch.

I shift Misti on to my other hip, trailing my spare hand around every surface I can find. Dusty window sills. Kitchen worktops. Table. Bookcase. In the bedroom, I trip on a heap of Misti's dolls and fall. The two of us topple sideways against the wardrobe, hard.

Misti's stopped screaming now. Her breath comes in huge, long gasps.

I sit on the bed and peel her arms and legs from round me. Her tiny fingers twist into the cloth of my sleeves, my hair. Her knees press into my waist.

'No, *noo-oh*,' she whispers. 'Bad, *bad*, Inky.'

'Misti, I need to find the torch,' I hiss. 'I need to find my school bag.'

Finally, I prise her free and fling her down on to the bed, sobbing.

I crash around the pitch-dark room, groping for my bag, the torch. I stumble next door to Mum's room, stub my toe on a suitcase, read every surface with my fingers like a blind girl. Soft chenille bedcover, plaited rag rug, splintery floorboards. In the distance, Misti's crying reaches fever pitch.

'It's OK, Misti,' I shout, more to comfort myself than her. 'I'm still here. I won't be long. I just have to find my bag . . .'

I crawl across the kitchen lino on hands and knees. Spilt lemonade. A drip of jam. Misti's old pyjamas, cold and wet.

No torch. No bag. My heart is thumping.

'*Ihhh-innn-keee!*' Misti howls.

In the bedroom again, my foot tangles up in Misti's tartan blanket. I drag it off the floor, wrap my little sister in its soft, safe warmth. I pull her on

154

to my lap and we sit for a long moment, heads touching, damp cheeks pressed together.

'I can't find it,' I tell her.

'I want Mummy,' she whispers back.

I try to think. I hoist her up again and we make slow progress through the dark flat. I bang my leg on the table, skid a little on felt pens scattered across the carpet. I pull open the door, and the cold air rushes in, but also the dim yellow light from the street lights round the front, the orange glow of the city sky.

I walk up the steps on to the gravel, shuffle round to the front of the house. No red Fiat. All the same, I carry Misti up the steps to the front door of 33 Hartington Drive, the tartan blanket trailing behind us like a dragon's tail. I find Ian's doorbell and lean on it.

Please be in. Please, please, please, be in. OK, so your car's not here, but let there be a miracle, please.

Nobody comes.

Next, I press Mrs Green's doorbell. She's in, I know. I can hear the loud canned laughter and phoney applause from some TV game show, the volume turned up high.

Please.

Nothing happens.

I come down the steps, crunch across the gravel, peer in through the tiny crack of light in Mrs

Green's curtains. She's asleep in her chair, her face falling sideways into the overstuffed chintz, the TV screaming at nobody.

I bang on the window. I scrunch my hand into a fist and hammer on the glass.

Mrs Green stirs, shifts around in the chair. A skeletal hand stretches out and knocks the TV remote to the floor. Her head lolls forward, white-haired, frail.

She's old. She's deaf. She can't hear us.

We stand on the gravel drive, stranded. I scan the upstairs windows for some sign of life. Everything is dark.

'I could ring Jane,' I whisper to Misti. 'She must be in by now.'

'Jane,' says Misti.

But I can't ring Jane, because I can't find my bag and the purse Jane gave me with the phone card, the number, the emergency cash. I can't ring anyone.

I can't fix the lights.

I can't stop Misti from crying silently into my shoulder.

I don't know what to do.

We sit on the back steps by the flat's open door for a very long time. I watch out for a red Fiat, a blue builder's van, a student on a bicycle from the middle flat. I wait to be rescued.

The last time I noticed the time, before the lights went out, it was past ten. It's much later now. Mum will be home soon. She said she wouldn't be long – she promised.

It may be early June, but it's freezing. Misti's hands and feet are like ice. A group of blokes walk down the street, shouting and laughing and kicking a tin can along the gutter. The pubs must be closing.

Mum won't be long.

Misti is shivering, her whole body shaking gently in my arms. Even in the yellow light from the street lamps, her face looks pale, her lips blue. I lift her up, my own hands and feet numb now from sitting so long. I take a long, last look along the drive, then walk down the steps into the pitch-black flat.

It must be very, very late.

I close the door.

My eyes struggle to make sense of the dark, and again I'm stumbling, shuffling. I make it to the nearest armchair, the one where we toasted our toes beside the fire just hours ago. We flop down into it.

Misti burrows into my neck.

'Bad, bad, Inky,' she breathes softly.

I pull the tartan blanket over us, and we fall into sleep.

27

Someone is hammering on the door, pressing the doorbell, banging on the glass.

I pull the blanket over my head, but the noise won't go away. It drags me out of sleep and back to reality.

Mum. She must have forgotten her key.

I haul Misti off my lap and leave her curled in the armchair, the tartan blanket around her.

'Mum?'

I navigate blindly towards the door, towards the banging. My fingers fumble with the doorhandle, the deadlock. I pull.

'Miss Collins?' says a woman's voice from the steps outside. 'Miss Collins, this is WPC Barrie. Could we come in?'

My body is cold all over. WPC Barrie?

'Miss Collins, is there a light?'

I stand in silence, in darkness, drifting.

'Is there a light?'

'No,' I manage to say at last. 'The powercard ran out. Nothing's working.'

WPC Barrie says something to the man behind her, and suddenly the broad, bright beam of a flashlight reaches into the flat. It lights up the felt pens, skewed across the carpet, the flowery Doc Marten boots Misti was playing with, the abandoned blue felt hat with the curling feather. Beyond them I can see my school bag, tucked neatly out of the way under the table.

The powercard, the phonecard, the emergency cash.

'Can we come in?' WPC Barrie asks, but they're in already, the flashlight sweeping across the carpet. It wakes Misti, who slides down from the chair and squints in the torchlight. In its bright beam, her face is filthy, streaked with jam and snot and tears.

WPC Barrie reaches down and lifts her up. 'Hello, pet,' she says. 'Oh, Lord – she's soaking wet. And worse. Oh, *yuk* . . .'

She picks up the tartan blanket and tries to wrap it round Misti, but my sister is crying again now, wriggling and scratching and biting.

'Inky!' she shrieks. '*Inkeeee!*'

I hold out my arms and WPC Barrie hands Misti over. She *is* soaking. She stinks.

'Miss Collins.' The policewoman puts a hand on

my arm. She clears her throat. 'I'm afraid there's been an accident. We have your mum down at the hospital. Now, she's OK, she's going to be *fine*, but she's very worried about you two. We're here to check . . .'

I press my face into Misti's hair, sticky with jam. I smell sugar, talc, the hot, sour reek of a full nappy, except there's no nappy there. I close my eyes tight shut and hug my baby sister.

The world spins and turns and we're alone in the dark.

'Indigo?' The policewoman puts an arm round my shoulders. 'Did you hear me? Is there anyone we can contact, anyone who can look after you?'

'Mum,' I whisper. 'I want my mum.'

WPC Barrie shakes her head. 'You can see your mum in the morning. She'll be well enough to see you then,' she says. 'Right now, though, we need to find a safe place for you two to stay overnight. Are there any relatives, friends, neighbours . . .?'

'*NO-OOO* . . .'

It can't be me screaming. I know I can't make such a loud noise. I wouldn't dare. I wouldn't want to be a nuisance, cause any trouble. So why are they staring at me like that? Why is Misti roaring and struggling and beating her fists against me?

White faces, dark peaked caps, strangers in the middle of our dark, musty flat.

'We're going to need Social Services,' the policeman says. 'Two hysterical kids, home alone, in a smelly, damp flat with no heat, no light. Look at the *state* of them.'

'Dave, give them a chance,' says the policewoman. 'They're bound to be distressed, aren't they? And there must be *someone*. Someone they can call.'

She keeps her arm round my shoulders, a hand stroking my hair. She whispers something soft and kind as she holds me, and slowly the panic subsides, the jagged pain dulls.

I'm still, now. I crouch, curled round Misti, trying to steady my breath, gather my thoughts.

'Indigo,' says the policewoman again. 'Is there anyone we can ring? Someone to look after you for a while? We can't leave you here alone.'

'I need to see my mum,' I say. 'I need to see her *now*.'

'That's not really possible,' the policewoman says. 'Tomorrow.'

'I need to see my mum,' I plead. 'Please. I have to. I *have* to see her.'

The two strangers exchange glances.

'We can see if that's possible,' WPC Barrie says at last. 'We can try. But first, we need a responsible adult, someone to look after you for a day or so.'

We stand on the front doorstep of 33 Hartington

Drive while the policeman pushes the bell for Ian's flat. No reply. There's no red Fiat, no Ian.

'Mrs Green?' I suggest, and they try her doorbell too. They rap on the glass. Her flat is dark now, and silent as the grave. I imagine her asleep, earplugs in to dull the sound of student parties overhead. Or lying awake, terrified to answer the door because it's the middle of the night.

'She's a bit deaf,' I explain. 'She's eighty-something.'

'That's no good,' says WPC Barrie. 'Anyone else?'

'Not really,' I say, but they try the bell for the student flat anyway. After a long wait, one of the balcony windows above creaks open and a grey, swaying figure appears. It says something very rude.

'Can you open up?' shouts WPC Barrie.

'What?' slurs the grey figure. 'What d'you want? We haven't done nothing, honest.'

An empty beer can clatters down from above, rattling across the gravel at our feet.

'Not a chance,' says the policeman. 'Hopeless.'

'Ring Jane,' I say. We dash back down to the flat and I grab my school bag, pulling out Jane's number. They call from the police car.

'Answerphone,' he says. 'I'll leave a message, but . . .'

We sit in the squad car and drive towards the hospital. WPC Barrie holds my hand in the dark. Misti, cocooned in soggy tartan, sleeps in my lap.

'Anyone else?' she asks me gently. 'Grandparents, aunts, uncles, cousins? Anyone we can call?'

'Gran lives in Wales,' I say.

'Do you know her phone number?' WPC Barrie asks.

I shake my head.

I pull my hand free of her grasp and reach down into my school bag. Phonecard, powercard, pound coins. My Victorian-project folder. Spelling jotter. Pencil case. Empty crisp packet.

At the bottom, dog-eared and creased, there's a fat, grubby envelope addressed to Gran. I never got around to buying a stamp. I hand the letter over.

'OK,' says WPC Barrie. 'Well done, Indigo. Well done.'

My mum is lying in a hospital bed, a tall bed made of shiny metal tubes and covered with a pale-blue waffle coverlet. She is wearing a white, short-sleeved nightie that ties behind her neck and looks like someone made it in a hurry from old sheets and white shoelaces.

She is propped up on huge white pillows, and she's smiling at me, but I can't smile back.

My face is frozen.

'Indie, love, iss OK . . .' she says, but her lips are swollen and black and held together with tiny slivers of white tape. The words come out all distorted.

My mum has plastic tubes stuck into her arm above her bandaged hand, bandages around her face, her chest, her body. There's a wad of white cotton taped over her left eye to hide the swelling and the stitches and the shiny, purple bruises. She has seven broken ribs, the nurse tells WPC Barrie, and a fractured jaw, and her left hand is crushed and badly bruised. Her fingers, purple, swollen sausages, flex slightly on the coverlet, the pale-blue sparkly nail varnish still perfect, unchipped.

I try to put my arms round her, but there's nowhere I can touch that doesn't hurt. A perfect tear rolls down her swollen cheek.

'Sorry, pet,' she whispers. 'I'm sorry.'

Then her eyes flicker shut and she turns her head away.

'Let her sleep,' WPC Barrie says. 'It's the best thing. Everything will look brighter in the morning.'

But it *is* the morning, four in the morning. The nurse finishes checking Mum's dressings, fiddles with the drip and switches off the light.

WPC Barrie shepherds me out into the hushed ward corridor. We walk noiselessly past the nurses' station, past the open doors to dimly lit rooms. We push through the heavy, swishing double doors and into the brightly lit foyer.

'What kind of an accident was it?' I ask WPC Barrie. 'Were they in the van? Was it a crash?'

Sitting on the sofa by the lift is a plump social worker called Lou. She cradles Misti in her lap, a tiny fair-haired refugee child wrapped in a tartan blanket. Lou smiles and nods as we approach.

She's *our* social worker now.

We never had one before.

'What happened?' I ask WPC Barrie again. 'Is Max OK? Is he hurt?'

She turns to look at me.

'Max Kelly isn't hurt, no,' she tells me gently. 'He's safe and well, locked in a police cell, down at the station. *He's* the person who did this to your mum, Indigo. It wasn't an accident. It was assault. If your mum will only press charges, he'll go to prison for it too.'

'Oh,' I say.

Misti sucks her fluffy rabbit and sleeps. Lou looks at me with sad, sympathetic eyes. WPC Barrie shrugs her shoulders, puts a hand on my sleeve.

I take a deep breath in.

Max.

What more is there to say?

I wake late, sandwiched between crisp pastel sheets in a room with mauve walls, purple carpet. The sun creeps through a gap in the pink ballerina curtains.

There's a soft knock at the door.

'Mmmm?'

The door opens and Misti crashes in, washed and brushed and dressed in a ruffled frock I've never seen before. She jumps on to the bed and hugs me.

'Inky! Come on, Inky . . .'

'No need to ask if you're awake now!'

A grey-haired woman, about Gran's age, stands in the doorway, smiling.

'I've run you a bath, love, and Lou's over at the flat getting you some clean clothes. We'll get you both fed and then Lou will get you to your Gran, and maybe back down to the hospital . . .'

I can remember the hospital, the policewoman, Lou. I remember Mum. I remember a taxi ride with Lou, then a nice, grey-haired lady in her dressing gown, fussing and smiling and tucking Misti up in a cot with high sides and clean, pastel blankets.

'Um . . . Auntie Kay?' I offer.

'That's right, love,' she beams. 'Now come on through and have that bath. I've put in plenty of bubbles.'

She's kind and friendly and thoughtful and sweet, but she's not my auntie. She's nothing to do with me. She's an emergency foster carer, somebody paid to take care of two lost, scared, filthy kids in the middle of the night.

First I have a social worker, now I have an emergency foster mum. And my own mum is lying in a hospital bed, with broken bones and blue-black bruises and a drip feeding liquid into her veins because the man who said he loved us beat her up.

She didn't fall. She didn't slip. She wasn't clumsy, and it wasn't an accident.

It was Max.

I always knew it, really. I just couldn't admit it, not even to myself.

I sit in the bath and splash bubbles about, listlessly. I slide under the water and wet my hair. I massage in shampoo that smells of oranges, then slip under the water again to rinse it off. I let my face sink down beneath the water, holding my breath, wondering what would happen if I never came up again.

Then I come up.

By the time I go downstairs, wrapped in a big towelling bathrobe, Lou is here with a bag of clothes from the flat. I get dressed, pick at some toast. Lou says we have an Emergency Case Meeting in town.

Auntie Kay tells us we're big, brave girls and ruffles our hair like she'll miss us. Lou says we won't be coming back to this neat little house with the ballerina bedroom and the bathroom that smells of steam and oranges and bubble bath. Gran is coming.

All I have to do is hang on till then.

So I keep it together all through the taxi ride, right through the walk across the quiet courtyard to the Social Services offices that are meant to be closed on Sundays. They're open, because of us. We're an emergency case. Our feet sink into soft carpet as we move along the corridor, Misti trailing her pink rabbit by its lone surviving ear.

Lou takes us to a sofa-stuffed waiting room, and there's a scrum and a racket and people are hugging me tight, stroking my hair, telling me to keep my chin up.

Jane is here, with Bob, her husband, and Ian from upstairs, and Mrs Green, and, amazingly, Miss McDougall from school in her best tweed suit and flouncy blouse. Everyone is talking at once. Jane says she's sorry she wasn't in last night; they went out for a meal after their shopping trip, had too much to drink and forgot to check the answerphone till morning.

'It's all my fault,' she says, her face pale and trembly.

'No,' I tell her. 'It's Max's.'

It doesn't matter that Ian drove down south to see his parents, that Mrs Green never answers the door after seven o'clock, that Miss McDougall thought it best not to ask too much about what was happening at home.

None of it matters, not now.

It's still Max's fault.

Lou ushers us through the waiting room and into an office, and then I don't have to hold it together any longer, because Gran is there. She folds us up in her arms, Misti and me both, and I'm crying now, letting out all the hurt and fear.

We sit on soft, plush chairs and answer questions while a man in a suit scribbles things down in a folder. Who is Max? Why was he out with Mum last night? Why were we home alone, in the dark and the cold?

Then Gran is signing papers and saying we'll be staying with her in Wales, me and Misti and Mum too. We'll have to stick around at the flat for a few days, till she's out of hospital and well enough to travel, but then we're out of here.

Lou shakes me by the hand and we're back to the waiting room and the people who care, want to help to make it better.

The adults scribble addresses, exchange scraps of paper.

'How he could *do* such a thing . . .'

'. . . no better than an animal . . .'

'If only I'd *known* those two girls were all alone . . .'

Then it's over, and we're away, safe at last in Gran's battered blue Volkswagen Beetle.

Gran leans back in the driver's seat and lets out a long, shuddery sigh. She pulls out the letter I wrote weeks back, unfolding the paper, looking at the untidy scrawl of words.

'Indie, I'm so sorry,' she says. 'The police gave me this letter earlier, and when I read it . . . Why didn't you post it, Indie, love?'

I shrug. 'Couldn't find a stamp.'

Gran puts a hand over her eyes. I notice suddenly that her hand is old, wrinkly, the veins sticking up like blue string.

'I had no idea,' she says. 'I worried when Anna didn't call, when she didn't return my calls, but Max kept telling me things were fine. Your mum *is* very independent, Indie, I know that. She can go for ages without getting in touch. Now I know why . . .'

Her pale-blue eyes blur with tears. 'I'm sorry you've had to cope alone. You're not alone now, pet. Not ever again, I promise.'

We hug. I rest my face against Gran's soft, papery cheek. At last, Misti gets bored and starts fiddling with the steering wheel. She honks the horn loudly, and we fall apart, grinning, grabbing seat belts.

Gran finds the key, turns it.

We're off.

We stay for five days in the damp basement flat, waiting till Mum is discharged from hospital. We visit every day. Her room fills up with flowers – posh roses and lilies from Jane, white lilac from Miss McDougall, peonies and irises and frothy snow-in-summer from Mrs Green, from the flower beds at number 33, the beds Mum weeded and dug and tidied.

Ian Turner doesn't send flowers – he thinks it was the bunch of flowers he gave Mum that made Max so mad in the first place. Mum's sure now that she caught a glimpse of Max in the super-market, that he followed us home and waited till he saw Ian leave.

Did he ever want to win Mum back, talk her round, make things right? Did he want us to be a family again? Mum thinks he did. But when she told him that she wasn't coming back, not ever, he got angry again. They argued in the restaurant, then later in the van. Max wouldn't take Mum home, wouldn't stop and let her out. She waited till he slowed for a traffic light, then jumped out of the van and tried to run. She slipped in her cute blue kitten heels and Max caught her, lashed out, lost it.

A passing car saw them and the driver called the police and ambulance on his mobile. When they got there, Mum says, Max was sitting at the side of the road, head in his hands. He didn't struggle as the police led him away.

'He didn't mean it,' I hear her tell Gran. 'He really didn't.'

Gran shakes her head. 'You have to press charges, Anna. You have to make him pay.'

Mum closes her eyes to end the conversation.

'What has he done to you, Anna Collins?' Gran asks, stroking the blonde curls that fall across Mum's bruised, swollen face. 'What has he done?'

I don't think she's talking about the broken bones.

When we're not at the hospital, we pack up the flat at 33 Hartington Drive. Gran says we won't be staying there a moment longer than we have to, and no wonder we're all so thin and pale. Mrs Green says we can store the boxes and furniture in her spare room for as long as we like, even though we're not coming back. Gran has been to the Housing Association and put our names down on a list for flats, and we get lots of points for being a single-parent family, temporarily homeless, and in crisis.

Gran says she's sure we'll have a flat by September.

'I'll miss you,' Mrs Green says.

'I'll miss you,' I say. I give her a big box of Thorntons dark-chocolate mints that Gran helped me buy, and I promise to visit once the summer is over and we're settled into our new flat.

Then, when Mum comes out of hospital, we drive down to Wales. We're going to spend the summer, not just a week like we usually do, but the whole long summer. And when the summer is over, Gran says Mum will be all better, and our flat will have come through – dry, clean, close to the schools.

'No mould, no damp,' she says.

'No bluebird bedroom, no Mrs Green,' I echo.

But it'll be better, all the same.

And now I'm in the middle of nowhere, the most beautiful bit of nowhere ever, Gran's cottage, just outside a tiny, pretty, Pembrokeshire village. Misti and I eat home-baked bread, warm from the Aga. We pick peas from the garden and eat them raw, popping the pods. We pick wild raspberries from the hedges, and eat them with thick, yellow cream and sprinkles of brown sugar.

We go to the village shop for butter and chocolate and comics. We feed Gran's tabby cat, Bronwen, and lie on the grass in the long back garden, shaded by towering foxgloves and wigwams of sweet peas.

In July, I get a parcel from Miss McDougall.

There are photos from the play, Aisha with her dark hair pushed up into a big, tweedy cap, raggedy clothes, singing her heart out. Jo as a flower seller, pretty in pink satin. Shane as Dodger, cheeky in a big top hat and tailcoat, blowing a kiss at the camera. There's a video too, a bit shaky and blurred in places, but I get to watch my friends sing and act and I manage to be glad for them, almost.

When I watch Aisha sing Oliver's sad solo, I can't help thinking it could have been me, wondering if I'd have had the guts to stand there in front of all those people. Aisha's brilliant, and the roar of applause when she stops singing is the closest to jealousy I get.

At the end of the tape, there's Mr Lennon giving a speech, thanking Miss McDougall, the parent helpers, the actors. 'And as for our star,' he says, 'all I can say is, take her home, Mrs Patel, and for goodness sake, feed her!' Everyone in the audience laughs and cheers.

The play was a sell-out, both nights, Miss

McDougall says. They're all sorry I couldn't be there.

Me too.

A week later, Aisha writes, four pages of pale-blue notepaper crammed with news and questions and stuff about school. She says they miss me, that it isn't the same without me, that Shane sends his love.

Jo misses you too, though she never says anything, Aisha says. But Jo seems like history. She used to be my friend – once.

Aisha sits in a desk on her own now, like before. She's waiting for me.

See you in September, Aisha writes. *At Kellway Comp!*

I write to Aisha and I write to thank Miss McDougall for the video. I send Mrs Green a postcard of the beach near Tenby, Jane a postcard of a sheep with mad, curly horns, and a cartoon postcard of a fire-breathing Welsh dragon to Ian.

In August, Mum gets the train home to stay with Jane for a few days. She's got an interview with the Housing Association about a flat, just off Calder's Lane. She signs the lease, goes along to see the supermarket people to ask whether they'll have her back in September, puts Misti's name down for a day nursery nearby. She rings and tells Gran the best news of all, that Max has put his house up for sale and done a flit. He's gone, this time for good.

When Mum comes back, we do holiday stuff. We go sailing, climb a real live mountain, take picnics down to the coast and eat ice lollies and paddle in the sea.

The summer slips by, and slowly the nightmare fades.

30

I'm up at seven, showered in record time. After a lifetime of navy pleated skirts and blue polo tops, I reach for a little grey skirt and a white top, an outsize black blazer with red braid trim. I brush my hair into high bunches, then pull it into little twists with the ends sticking out all jaggedy. I resist the temptation to chew at my fingernails. They're short and neat and painted 'Palest Peach' (in case the teachers are going to be strict about that kind of thing).

I have a new pencil case, new felts, new ruler, pencils and pens. I have a new school bag, a big black backpack that fastens with a wide, diagonal strap across my body. I look in the full-length mirror in the pine wardrobe door. It could be worse. I feel grown-up and five years old, both at the same time.

Mum's in the pine kitchen-diner, dishing up muesli and chopped strawberries. Misti balances on the edge of a chair, still pink and pyjamaed, stealing the ripest ones.

I splash on cold milk and eat a few spoonfuls, anxiously.

'You look great,' Mum says. 'So grown-up.'

And I feel it, even though I know we'll be the littlest kids at school now, lost, out of our depth, squeaky clean, marked out by our shiny new shoes and freshly ironed uniforms.

I wonder if I'll miss Calder's Lane Primary with its rumbling radiators and corridors that smell of disinfectant and boiled cabbage. Can you get nostalgic for school stew, bumped knees dabbed with witch hazel, spelling tests and chalk dust? You can. *I* can.

I wonder who'll be sitting in my old desk this morning, under Miss McDougall's eagle eye.

She wasn't so bad, in the end. For a teacher.

The doorbell rings. It's a bright, loud burst of sound, a million miles from the long, reedy peal at 33 Hartington Drive.

'That'll be Aisha,' I say. 'She said she'd call over. I'll be off now, then.'

'OK. Bye, love,' Mum says, hugging me. 'Good luck.'

'Good luck, Inky,' Misti says, hugging my legs.

I open the door, and Aisha's grin lights up the little lobby. I spoke to her last night on the phone, but this is the first time we've got to see each other. We only made it back from Wales yesterday afternoon.

'Missed you,' Aisha says.

'Missed *you*,' I echo shyly.

'Hello, Aisha,' Mum calls. 'Take care, girls. Be good!'

'We will!' Aisha laughs, and she hooks her arm through mine and walks me away. The door clicks shut behind me and we clatter down the steps.

'Scared?' Aisha asks.

'Nah,' I bluster. 'Course not.'

We walk in silence, then turn to each other, pulling terrified faces.

'OK, I'm scared,' I laugh. 'Petrified.'

'Me too,' Aisha admits. 'You look great, though. All sort of rosy-cheeked and healthy. D'you think you'll miss Wales?'

I will, I know. I'll miss Gran, and the cottage, and the warm bread and the home-made jam. I'll miss the way it felt safe and steady and picture-book perfect, and how all of us, Mum, me and Misti, learned to relax, let go and breathe again.

'A bit,' I say cautiously. 'But it's good to be back. The flat's amazing.'

We're in a Housing Association flat, and though we've only just moved in for real, and it's still all boxes and bin bags and clutter, it's heaven after

Hartington Drive. It's smaller, but it's also clean, dry, warm and modern. The doors and cupboards and built-in wardrobes are honey-coloured pine. The floors are carpeted, wall-to-wall, with soft green carpet. The windows are double-glazed and there's central heating, and we've got a phone and a shower and a small, second-hand TV. Mum's saving up for a video player too. She reckons we'll have it by Christmas. She starts back at the supermarket next week, and Misti's starting Nursery. We won't have to scrimp and save any more.

'I think your flat's kind of like ours,' Aisha is saying. 'We're only round the corner, and they're both Housing Association, aren't they? I mean, it won't be as cool and arty as the basement flat ... remember the flowers and the bluebirds your mum painted all around the wall in the bedroom?'

'I know. It *was* beautiful. Mum's going to do a mural in our new room too. It's going to be a rainbow, arching right across the corner, and a big, spirally, yellow sunshine with wiggly rays.'

'Wow! How come your mum's so cool? I'm not even allowed so much as one measly Eminem poster in *my* room,' Aisha moans.

'That's because your mum is trying to save you from yourself,' I point out. 'I mean, Eminem – yeeuchh!'

Aisha whacks me with her school bag and we fall about laughing.

'What's wrong with him?' she demands. 'It's a free country. Just cos he doesn't have sandy hair and travel by skateboard!'

'Aisha!' I protest, but she fixes me with a stare and I give up trying to argue, shrugging, grinning.

She fishes a bundle of strawberry laces out of her pocket and divides them up.

'How's your mum?' she asks.

I concentrate on my strawberry lace. This is a question that Jo would never have asked. We didn't do deep and meaningful, Jo and I. We did giggles and fun and jokes, and nothing ever got gloomy and sad. Except that when we couldn't keep the giggles going, the whole friendship fell to pieces. I stopped pretending that everything was fine, and Jo stopped being my best mate.

Aisha wrote me five letters over the summer. Jo didn't write any.

There's more to life than giggles and make-believe.

'Mum's OK,' I say thoughtfully. 'I mean, she's got a scar on her face, but you'd never notice it. Not really. And I think, at last, she's over Max. She didn't press charges in the end. Max wrote to Mum and told her he's living in Brighton, setting up in business with his brother. He said he was sorry. Mum chucked the letter into Gran's Aga.'

'Wow,' Aisha says.

I shrug. I hope things work out for Mum, of course I do. Sometimes I dream of Ian Turner and nights in with daft videos and takeaway pizzas, but mostly I just feel glad that Max is gone, for good. Mum has to find her own happy ending, I know that much. I can't do it for her.

'She doesn't wear blue any more,' I tell Aisha. 'Not all the time, anyway. She reckons that fortune-teller got it all wrong. She went shopping with Gran last week, and she bought a purple top and green suede boots and a big Oxfam-shop jumper with rainbow stripes.'

'Maybe that'll be lucky for her, then, all the colours of the rainbow,' says Aisha.

'Maybe.'

As we get closer to Kellway Comp, the streets fill up with kids. Nobody wants to be late, especially not on the first day of term. And we're dawdling, Aisha and I, catching up on three whole months of stuff.

We stop on the corner to share the last strawberry lace. Up ahead, a queue of double-decker buses spills teenagers out on to the pavement by the gates of the high school. Cars stop and crispy-new Year Sevens emerge, looking startled.

Giant-sized Year Elevens mooch along, looking bored and cool and vaguely crumpled.

'Hiya.'

A couple of Year Seven boys lope towards us, almost unrecognizable in perfect black blazers and new-term haircuts. Iqbal – and Shane.

Aisha elbows me in the ribs.

'He's *walking*!' she squeaks.

'Hiya, Shane, Iqbal,' I say, pretending to be more interested in the strawberry lace. I can't hide my grin, though. And my heart is thumping.

Shane and Iqbal walk past, swaggering a bit. There, laced tightly on to the back of Shane's brand-new backpack, is his battered old skateboard, rainbow bright.

He looks back, grinning, and winks at me, and my insides turn to melted chocolate.

It's good to be back.

As Aisha and I turn into the school gate, we see a small, brown-haired girl in an outsize blazer standing alone beside the huge sign that says *Kellway Comprehensive*. Her eyes scan the rabble of kids, searching through the faces, biting her lip. She looks very young, very lost, alone.

'Hi, Jo,' I say.

We stop, uncertain, and the tide of students flows right on round us, bumping our elbows, knocking our school bags.

'I was waiting for you,' Jo says.

'Right.'

She stares at her feet. Shiny black lace-ups, fancy white socks. Then she looks up, right at me.

'I want to say sorry,' she says quietly. 'I was rotten to you last term, stupid and mean and self-ish. I – I don't know what happened, but I know things went wrong, and I wasn't there for you.'

'No,' I say slowly. 'No, you weren't.'

'Indie, I've been a useless mate, but I'm sorry, I really am,' she says. 'Will you give me another chance?'

I look at Aisha, and Aisha looks away. It's my call.

Aisha is a better mate than Jo ever was, someone I can trust, someone I can really talk to. She knows stuff about my life that Jo never even thought of asking. She's my best friend. Somehow, I think she always will be.

But don't you need all the friends you can get?

I smile at Jo and give her the tail end of my last strawberry lace. Across the busy playground, the school bell rings out, loud and jangly and persistent.

I link arms with Jo, and Aisha grabs my other arm, squeezing it softly.

'Come *on*,' she says. 'We're going to be late . . .'

BEST FRIENDS are there for you in the good times and the bad. They can keep a secret and understand the healing power of chocolate.

BEST FRIENDS make you laugh and make you happy. They are there when things go wrong, and never expect any thanks.

BEST FRIENDS are forever,

BEST FRIENDS ROCK!

cathy cassidy's
My Best Friend
Rocks!
enter at
cathycassidy.com
mizz
award

IS YOUR BEST FRIEND ONE IN A MILLION?
Go to **cathycassidy.com**
to find out how you can show your
best friend how much you care